pearl

pearl

Jo Knowles

Henry Holt and Company
New York

Acknowledgments

I'd like to give a huge thanks once again to my fearless writing partners, Cindy Faughnan and Debbi Michiko Florence. I'll meet you anywhere you want. Also thanks to Robin Wasserman, for her brilliant insight and enthusiasm, and to Andrea Beaty, for wanting the recipe. Thanks to my editor, Kate Farrell, for falling in love with a girl called Bean, and to my agent, Barry Goldblatt, for believing in her. And finally, as always, I owe my biggest thanks to my husband, Peter, for everything.

· · ● ● ● ● ● · ·

YA
Knowles.
Johanna

Henry Holt and Company, LLC
Publishers since 1866
175 Fifth Avenue
New York, New York 10010
macteenbooks.com

Henry Holt® is a registered trademark of Henry Holt and Company, LLC.
Text copyright © 2011 by Jo Knowles

Library of Congress Cataloging-in-Publication Data
Knowles, Johanna (Johanna Beth).
Pearl / Jo Kowles.—1st ed.
p.   cm.
Summary: After fifteen-year-old Bean's beloved grandfather Gus dies, she discovers uncomfortable secrets about him, her mother, and the father she has never known.
ISBN 978-0-8050-9207-3
[1. Family problems—Fiction.   2. Lesbians—Fiction.   3. Emotional problems— Fiction.   4. Best friends—Fiction.   5. Friendship—Fiction.   6. Mothers and daughters— Fiction.]   I. Title.
PZ7.K7621Pe 2011   [Fic]—dc22   2010029883

First Edition—2011
Book designed by Elizabeth Tardiff
Printed in the United States of America

1   3   5   7   9   10   8   6   4   2

For Peter and Eli—my dreamers, my believers,

my best friends, my family. I love you.

pearl

chapter one

Henry and I get comfortable in our usual *Days of Our Non Lives* positions on his mother's scratchy plaid couch in their tiny living room. We're just in time for the familiar hourglass. Sally hushes us for the opening voice-over.

Like sands through the hourglass . . .

Henry and I look at each other and telepathically exchange a single, familiar phrase: *We are pathetic.*

. . . so are the days of our lives.

The small air conditioner duct-taped into the only window in the cramped living room hums mournfully over the tragedy about to play out on the TV, as well as the sagging couch the three of us sit on—Sally in the middle, as always. I close my eyes and feel the cool air against my sweaty face as the opening scene starts.

Sally leans forward to watch. Her huge breasts rub over the top of the metal mixing bowl filled with Doritos she holds in her lap. She grips the edges of the bowl, her dimpled arms blocking Henry and me from reaching in to grab a chip, as if we don't know the rule or might try to break it: *No eating during* Days. Sally says the crunching is too distracting. Instead, we wait for the commercials and crunch during the ads while Sally fills us in on whatever we've missed since the last episode we watched with her. Her face always gets a warm glow when she talks about TV love, like it's going to ooze into her own life any day now. Sally believes with every molecule that makes up her large pink body that somewhere out there is the perfect man for her. Henry always looks sad when his mom says this. Neither of us believes it. Even if that man did exist, how could he find Sally when she never leaves the house? There is only one man who knows where Sally is, and he left fifteen years ago, two months after Henry was born.

Henry doesn't know much more about his father than I know about mine, and maybe that's how we got to be such good friends, sharing our soap-opera-like dreams about who our real fathers are and how they might come back into our lives. The only things I know about my father are the hints I get from listening at closed doors. Not that I get that many opportunities. But sometimes, when my mom comes home particularly late from her waitressing job, I can get lucky. Whenever she's late, it means she's spent her extra tips at the bar on half-priced booze. If her keys jingle in the lock for more than fifteen seconds, I know it's a night to listen for information. The first thing my mom does after going to the bathroom is head to her bedroom and call her best friend, Claire, to recap the last fifteen years of her life and all the places it's gone wrong.

One night three years ago, the keys were jingling in the lock for nearly a full minute before I heard Gus, my grandfather, rush down the hall. As soon as his footsteps thundered down the stairs, I inched out of my room to the top of the stairs to listen.

"Where the hell have you been?" he roared when he opened the door for her. "Have you forgotten you have a twelve-year-old daughter upstairs? Have you forgotten how she came to be?"

"I haven't forgotten," my mom said in the resentful voice she used when she talked to him. "I haven't forgotten that *it wasn't my fault!*"

Gus gave a doubting grunt.

"You think I *asked* for it? You think I *wanted* to be attacked?" My mom's voice shook with anger and drunkenness.

"I don't know what you expect, Lexie. I don't know what you ever expected. You come out of work late every night, drunk, dressed like—"

"Don't. Don't you dare!"

"I'm asking you, Lexie. What the hell did you expect?"

I leaned farther over the stairs, waiting for my mom to reply. I hated it when they fought, which was practically every time they were in the same room. Luckily, that wasn't very often if they could help it.

"Nothing," she finally said almost in a whisper. "I didn't expect a goddamned thing."

I scooted back to my room as soon as she neared the stairs, then pressed my ear against the wall that separated our bedrooms.

"Damn that Bill. Damn him to hell!" she kept crying on her side of the wall. She was telling Claire all about the horrible things Gus had implied. "That bastard thinks I *wanted* to get pregnant?" she asked.

I can still remember how her words punched my chest. I quickly tried to piece them together, hoping some image of the truth might emerge. *Attacked. Pregnant. Bill. Twelve years.* But there were still too many missing pieces.

Up until then, Henry and I had been pretty satisfied with the stories we'd concocted about our dads. Mine was a pilot who disappeared in the Bermuda Triangle. Henry's had been kidnapped by terrorists. These scenarios were a lot more interesting than the unsatisfactory ones our moms fed us up to that point: My dad was simply a "mistake" and better off gone, and Henry's dad "disappeared" when he was still a baby. We needed our dads to have names and lives, and—most important—futures with us. I wasn't expecting the story about Bill.

The next morning I crept into my mom's room and gently woke her up. Her eyes were puffy from crying, and she smelled like hangover.

"Who's my father?" I asked her, trying to sound like I meant business. "Tell me who Bill is."

"What? How?"

"I heard you," I told her. "Last night. I know his name is Bill, and I want to know who he is."

She closed her eyes for a minute, then opened them again and looked me straight in the face. "Please don't ask me about him. Please don't say that name." She rolled over and put her pillow over her head.

"Is he my dad? Where is he?"

She lifted the pillow. "Some things are better left unsaid," she said to the wall. "Trust me."

"I have a right to know," I told her.

She put the pillow back over her head. "There's nothing to tell," she mumbled into the pillow.

"Liar," I whispered.

"I heard that! And stop listening in on my phone calls!"

I left her and went to my room where I shut my door, got back into bed, and put my own pillow over my head. Later, when I told Henry what had happened, he was as disappointed as I was. I selfishly suspected it was because he realized if the father we'd invented for me could turn out to be a sham, so could his.

When the phone rings, Sally motions for Henry to answer even though the only people who call here are me and telemarketers, and I'm sure Henry would prefer to just let the machine pick up. Sally refuses to be put on the Do Not Call list. I think it's because she's so lonely she actually likes to have a chat, even if it pains her to refuse to give money after the five-minute spiel she's just been patient enough to listen to.

Henry grabs the phone off the coffee table and heads down the hallway so Sally's show won't be interrupted. As soon as the door to his room clicks shut, a commercial comes on.

Sally and I reach for a handful of Doritos and crunch quietly. Then we reach in again. My orange fingers collide with the back of her puffy white hand, leaving an orange print. She pretends not to notice. We're crunching through a Jenny Craig ad when Henry returns.

"That was your mom, Beany," he says casually. "She says come home she has something to tell you."

"My *mom*?" I ask. Never, in the history of our friendship, has my mom *ever* called me at Henry's house. I didn't even know she knew Henry's last name to look up his number.

Henry shrugs, failing to recognize the significance.

"Come with me," I say.

He looks at the rattling air conditioner longingly, but nods okay. Sally's show is back on so it's understood we don't need to say good-bye. We leave the cool cave of their living room and step into the blinding, baking sun.

Henry wipes his forehead with the back of his hand and pulls his T-shirt away from his body as we trudge along. He has a thing about sweat spots. Even though he puts two layers of deodorant on, he still sweats through three shirts a day in the summer. He says he must have inherited overactive sweat glands from his father because Sally never sweats. I don't point out that Sally never moves enough to work up a sweat in the first place.

"Why would my mom call me?" I ask him for the third time.

Henry shrugs and fans his shirt.

We walk the rest of the familiar two blocks in silence, except for the steady smack of my flip-flops sticking to my sweaty feet and Henry huffing disagreeably, flapping his T-shirt. The old, run-down houses that line the street are quiet in the still, hot summer air. Time seems to have stopped thirty years ago on our road. Gus says ever since the economy tanked in the late eighties and the rich people moved out, the neighborhood has gone to seed. There are just a handful of old folks from his day who still live here. The rest are from "away" as he likes to say.

As we walk, I look at each house, thinking about the stories Henry and I have made up about each family living inside. When we get to my house, I think about the real stories it holds, and wonder what new drama my mom is about to add to it.

This can't be good is all I can figure.

chapter two

When we get to the paint-chipped front steps of my house, Henry moves closer to me. I can smell his deodorant and the fabric softener Sally uses because she likes the little teddy bear in the ads. I move closer too, so that our arms touch.

Being close to Henry has always made me feel safe. Ever since I met him at the MiniMart on the corner of our street. I was there to buy my mom some ginger ale for her hangover and get myself a treat with the change. Henry was buying his mom *Soap Opera Digest* and some Suzy Q's. We were seven and it was July. Sally said later this was a sign, us being seven and meeting in the seventh month. She said we were meant to be friends forever.

That first day, Henry and I stepped out of the MiniMart together and began to walk home, side by side.

"What's your name?" he asked shyly.

"Bean," I said. At school everyone called me by my real name, Pearl. But right away, I knew Henry wasn't like everyone else.

"*Bean*. As in the vegetable?"

"Actually, it's a legume."

He gave me a weird look. I just shrugged. I knew it was a stupid name, but it was what I'd always been. My mom said she named me Pearl because I was her unexpected gem. But I don't think pearls are actually gems. And I don't think I'm one, either. Gus said the first time he held me, I felt soft and squishy like a bean, not hard and cold like a pearl. But I personally believed the real reason he wouldn't call me Pearl was because it was the name my mom chose.

"I'm Henry," Henry said. I thought he might hold his hand out to me for a shake, only he couldn't because he had a plastic bag in each hand.

On our way home, we stayed side by side. We discovered that we would be in the same class in the fall and that we lived only two blocks from each other. By the time we reached his house, I felt like I had my first real friend.

Unlike Sally, my mom never paid much attention to Henry and me and our fated friendship. She also never seemed to notice that Henry was my *only* friend. She never commented on the fact that I didn't have any girls come over for what other parents called "playdates." Or that I was never invited to sleepovers or birthday parties. My mom never signed me up for soccer or swimming lessons or Girl Scouts or any of the other things the rest of the girls did in my classes. I'd eagerly hand her the permission slips sent home in my folders from school, but she just scoffed, wondering who had time to trek their kids all over town. My mom always said there was no such thing as a normal childhood and that I should be glad I wasn't having one. But I think that was just her pathetic attempt to make my pitiful lack of a social life—and her disinterest in helping me get one—into something resembling cool. It was also her way of avoiding all the other moms, who were at least ten years older than her.

Behind her back, I'd ask Gus to take me. I remember the first Girl Scout meeting I went to, and how all the other girls' moms came into the host's house to pick them up. The host mom made them coffee, and they stood around in the kitchen and gossiped and complained about their husbands. When Gus came to get me, all the moms gave each other the eye, which I was pretty sure was their way of saying, "Poor Pearl. Her mom had her when she was fifteen and never married. I guess we *could* have it a lot worse." And I swear all the girls looked at me in the same pitying way their moms did.

The truth is, I was better off with Henry. I didn't need to play soccer or learn how to make a sit-upon to use when I went camping in the woods. Because no one was ever going to take me camping in the first place. I didn't need badges or trophies. Just a friend.

I pause on the front porch before opening the screen door. Henry stops, too. We look at each other just for a second, then Henry gives me a "let's get this over with" nod and opens the door for me.

Inside, I smell tomato sauce cooking. This is not a good sign. Whenever my mom is nervous or upset, she cooks. Unless it's nighttime. Then she drinks.

As we walk down the hall to the kitchen, I peek into the living room to say hi to Gus, but his chair is empty, which means he's out fishing or taking a nap—the two activities he always resorts to when my mom is home during the day. The sunken spot molded to his sagging body makes me feel lonely.

This morning when I left for Henry's, Gus was sitting there reading the paper. When I stopped to say good-bye to him, he looked up and sighed at me in his sad way. "Be good, Bean," he said, just like always. *Be good.* As if I've ever gotten into anything resembling trouble in my entire so-called life. Now that I'm the age my mom was when she had me, I know what he really means. *Don't be like your mother.*

Henry and I make our way to the kitchen and the sounds and smells of cooking. My mom stands at the stove with her back to us. Her hair is tied in her waitress pony-tail. She looks about eighteen, not thirty. I think whoever my dad was must have been a real scag because my mom is tall and beautiful and I am short and plain. The only clue I have to what my father looked like is by looking in the mirror, which I try to avoid at all costs.

I am no Pearl.

My mom turns around when we enter the kitchen.

"Sit down, Bean girl," she says, turning back to the pot.

I don't want to sit down.

Henry pulls out a chair from the kitchen table in the corner of the room, but he doesn't sit, either.

"What's going on?" I ask.

Her back rises and falls slowly as she takes a deep breath. The ends of her ponytail curl up in a perky way, but the wisps of hair falling on the side of her face show how worn out she really is.

She has a tank top on under her apron. She's also wearing the cutoff jeans shorts that Gus says make her look "loose." I hate that word. When she turns back to face me again, the front of the apron covers her shorts so it looks like she isn't wearing anything underneath. She keeps stirring the pot, even though she has to reach behind her to do it. The sauce bubbles. She wipes the sweat off her forehead with the back of her other arm.

"Okay," she says. "I'm just going to tell you."

But instead she keeps stirring and staring at me.

"What?" I finally ask.

"Gus is dead," she says, just as if she's saying "I have to work late tonight."

"Huh?" I say. I shake my head as if I have water in my ears and misunderstood.

She turns back to the pot and reaches for the pepper grinder, which she carefully turns above the bubbling sauce, sprinkling a fine, gray dust into the pot.

"Mom! Would you just stop for two seconds! What's going on?"

I step closer and pause, remembering Gus's empty chair in the living room.

"Wait," I say. "Where's Gus?"

My mom looks up at the ceiling.

"I called at the bottom of the stairs when it was time for lunch and he didn't come down. I kept calling, yelling at him." She shakes her head. "I called him a bastard under my breath," she says quietly. "But he still didn't answer me. So I finally went up and found him there. In bed. Dead."

The sweat on my forehead starts to drip down my temple. Henry breathes behind me. It is stifling in this kitchen.

"Are—are you sure?" I finally ask.

"Yes, Beany. I'm sure."

"But, then—" I see him in the living room this morning, looking up at me from his paper.

Be good.

I stand in the kitchen with the simmering pot as the prickles of truth start at my toes and make their way all the way up to my heart. My lip quivers. I bite it still.

"Where—where is he now?" I ask, trying to steady my voice. I don't know why I don't want to cry. It's what normal people would do when they find out their grandfather's dead. But . . . we aren't normal.

My mom looks at the ceiling, up toward his room, as she stirs the pot. I follow her gaze.

Gus is dead. Gus is gone. I imagine his still body above us. Alone. The prickles begin to feel like knives.

I don't move. I just stand still and let the pain cut deep.

My mom stops looking at the ceiling and stares into the sauce, as if the bits of basil are tea leaves she can read our future from. Then, slowly, the wooden spoon slips from her hand into the sauce and disappears in the red as my mom sinks to the linoleum floor. She covers her face with her hands and brings her knees up to her chest like a little kid.

I slowly walk over to her and kneel next to her. I feel clumsy. I can't remember the last time I touched her. But I manage to put my arms around her sweaty body and hug her awkwardly. She leans into me and sobs. She smells like garlic and sweet basil and tarragon. I hold tight, afraid she'll tip over if I let go. She feels uncomfortable and unfamiliar, and I wish it was her arms around me, instead.

After a while she stops crying and moves out of my arms. She leans against the oven door and covers her face so I can't see the proof that she ever cared about Gus. Henry pushes the chair I didn't use back in. His soft footsteps creak gently across the floor and into the living room. My mom looks up at the sound of his voice reciting our name and address.

"I'm so sorry, Bean," she says. "I know how much you loved him."

But she doesn't hug me or hold me or let me cry into her the way I imagine she should. She just looks at me through her watery eyes and shakes her head. "I can't believe he's gone."

When the police and the paramedics arrive, an officer helps my mom off the floor and asks where Gus is. I look away when the paramedics carry him out on the stretcher, even though I'm sure they've covered his face with a sheet, like on TV. I don't want to risk seeing his still shape.

When they're gone, my mom turns to Henry. "Make me a drink?" she asks.

Henry looks confused, but finds the vodka my mom keeps in the freezer and pours it over some ice, then adds some orange juice. We've seen her do this at least a hundred times.

"Lexie?"

The screen door in the front hall whines open and footsteps rush toward us.

"Oh, honey." Claire wraps her skinny arms around my mom. Standing above her, Claire presses my mom's head into her stomach and pats it like she's a child. My mom moves her hands around Claire's small waist and holds on, burying her face in Claire's middle.

Claire picks up my mom's glass and takes a long drink from it.

"Could you two leave us alone a minute?" she asks Henry and me. My mom pulls her head away from Claire. She looks even younger than me, with the wisps of hair, wet with sweat and tears, clinging to her face. She nods at us, confirming we should get out.

In the living room, we sit side by side on the sofa, facing the empty chair with Gus's indent on it. We stare at the quiet gray TV screen. *General Hospital* is probably on by now. If Gus was here, he'd be reading the paper. If I turned on the TV, he would rustle the pages in disapproval. Then I would turn it off and ask him what was happening in the real world. And he would tell me about people blowing each other up in the Middle East. And shake his head. And I would think TV life was preferable. But I wouldn't say anything. I might even lean over and touch his hand. Instead, I lean over and touch the empty arm of the chair, worn almost to the bone.

Be good. Be good. It's all I can hear. I keep trying to feel something, but my body feels like a silent echo. I feel like that chair. Like the weight of loss has made me all out of shape and ugly.

Every so often we hear the scrape of a chair sliding across linoleum—Claire getting up to refill my mom's glass.

"You can cry, ya know," Henry says when I lean back to close my eyes against the sound.

"I know," I say back.

And then I do.

chapter three

The next morning I get out of bed and listen for the usual sound of the news coming from the TV in Gus's room.

Then I remember.

In the hallway, all the doors but mine and the one to the upstairs bathroom are closed. I walk down the faded and worn Oriental runner in the hallway and stand outside Gus's door, listening. When I was younger I used to knock on his door if I heard the news on inside. He'd let me sit on my grandmother's old rocker and we'd watch together. Sometimes he'd let me change to a cartoon and he'd pretend to laugh even though I think he personally hated those shows.

I open the door carefully. The bed is made and both windows are open. The curtains that have been there since before I was born—since before my grandmother died, I bet—blow in the morning breeze. The air smells like hot, cut grass from outdoors mixed with polished wood and folded wool blankets. And memories.

On the dresser there's a single, silver-framed black-and-white photo of my grandparents. My grandmother died before I was born, when my mom was younger than I am now. But I've always felt like I knew her. Gus told me story after story about the special way she cut onions, roasted peppers, stacked lasagna with homemade noodles he'd helped her roll out with her old, hand-crank pasta maker that my mom still uses on special occasions. He'd tell me how she would spend hours in the kitchen with my mom, teaching her all her secret cooking tips. Gus described these to me in detail, knowing my mom would never bother to share them with me.

"Never learn to cook," she always says, "or you'll be cooking for people the rest of your life."

My mom is the most depressing person I know.

I pick up the photo and study Gus's smiling eyes and try to remember the last time I saw him look truly happy.

When I was little, Gus took me fishing out on the stinky river behind our house. He would tell me fishing stories about him and my grandmother and make me laugh. He'd hold my hand when we crossed the street. He'd cut my food into tinier pieces than my mom had, so I wouldn't choke. He shined my Mary Janes for picture day at school, even though the shoes wouldn't be in the picture.

Muffled laughter comes from my mom's bedroom. Claire and my mom. God, it's like they're twelve and having a stupid pajama party. Of course, my mom probably *was* twelve the last time she had a friend stay over. Getting pregnant with me pretty much took care of her social life. But honestly, they seem far too happy for this occasion. I would really like to know what's so funny.

I take the photo of my grandparents and walk back to my room, leaving Gus's door open.

More giggles come crackling down the hall, paired with the padding of slippered feet. I quickly jump into bed and crawl under my covers, pretending to be asleep.

"I thought I shut this," my mom says.

There's a click.

"He's haunting me already."

"Stay in there, you old coot," says Claire.

"You're awful!" my mom says, giggling again.

Their footsteps pause in my open doorway.

"Should we get her up? It's going to be a busy day."

"Nah, let her sleep," my mom says. "There's not much for her to do."

They move on along the hall and down the stairs. I study the framed photo again and wonder what my grandmother was like. I wonder if she braided my mom's hair and read her bedtime stories like regular moms do. I wonder if she let my mom have friends over and go to birthday parties and join clubs and sports and do all the other things normal kids get to do. If she kissed my mom good night at bedtime, or hugged her when she was sad. And if she would have done the same to me, if she was here now.

In my sock drawer, I find the tiny velvet box Gus gave to me for my thirteenth birthday. Inside, there are two tiny pearl earrings that belonged to my grandmother, and that she wears in the photo.

The night Gus gave them to me, my mom had made us a special dinner and we were sitting at our usual seats around the dining room table. I opened my mom's gift first, which was a flat box I was sure was a gift certificate to the mall disguised as a book. But when I picked it up to do the usual shake, it was too heavy for a plastic card. As I slowly tore the wrapping paper, my mom bit her bottom lip while Gus acted uninterested. Inside the box was a book wrapped in pink tissue paper. A journal. A plain old black composition book like they sell at the MiniMart. Wow. How thoughtful.

"Do you like it, Beany?" my mom had asked.

I smiled and nodded, even though I was disappointed. What would I write in a journal, anyway? I lived the most boring life on the planet.

"I always had a journal when I was a teenager." She glanced at Gus who looked away. I wished for just one night they could try to like each other. If we couldn't be a normal family, at least we could be a pleasant one. Just for my birthday.

"Anyway, I thought you might like one, too," she said.

"It's great, Mom," I lied, putting it back in the box. "Thanks."

Then Gus handed me a much smaller box and cleared

his throat. I glanced at my mom, who looked bored, but curious.

I carefully removed the wrapping to find an old velvet box. When I opened the lid, the tiny hinges creaked a little. Inside, were two very small pearl earrings. Gus had never given me jewelry before, and I felt kind of embarrassed. Even though my mom had taken me to have my ears pierced, I never remembered to change my earrings and pretty much just wore the silver studs I had my ears pierced with.

"They belonged to your grandmother," Gus said. "And I know she would want you to have them."

I touched the tiny pearls with my fingers. "They're beautiful," I said. "Thank you."

"Pearls were your grandmother's favorite," Gus said quietly. "I gave those to her for our tenth wedding anniversary." He sat back in his chair and blinked his watery eyes.

My mom got up and cleared our dessert dishes without commenting. She never talked about my grandmother. But I wondered then if that was the real reason she named me Pearl. Maybe she wanted my name to be some sort of reminder.

"What was she like?" I asked Gus for the thousandth time.

He sat forward again and looked at the box in my hands. "Like no one else," he said from someplace far away.

I could hear how much he missed her, and I felt bad for reminding him. I didn't know what to say, so I reached over and put my hand on his. The back of his hand felt cold and wrinkled, and I was glad when he slowly pulled it away.

Even though I wanted to, I didn't dare put the pearls in my ears. They were so small and delicate. And they didn't feel like mine. Instead, I just held the small box. We waited for my mom to come back from clearing the dishes, but she didn't. Finally, I took my two presents upstairs. I flipped through the empty pages of the journal and knew I would never be able to fill them. Journals were for writing your secrets in. For describing your life and your loves. And I didn't have any of those things. Instead, I put it in my sock drawer, along with the earrings. Then Henry called to wish me a happy birthday. And then, I guess I must have just gone to bed.

Every so often, I would take the earrings out of my drawer and look at them, but I never wore them. I would just touch them, and wish for the thousandth, maybe the millionth time, that I'd known my grandmother.

Now, I touch the tiny earrings again. I lift the flap they're set in so I can take off the backings and put them on for the first time. It's been a while since I wore any earrings at all and they feel strange in my ears, as if they don't really belong.

I pick up the picture frame again and touch my grandparents' faces through the glass. I try to smile back at them, but my mouth won't let me. Instead, I hold them against my chest, my heart, and close my eyes, trying to shut out the sounds of my mom and Claire laughing downstairs.

chapter four

In the kitchen, Claire and my mom sit at the tiny table with mugs of coffee and a notepad.

"We're planning the funeral," my mom says.

Claire is drinking from my favorite mug.

"Where are we having it?" I ask.

"At the river," my mom says. "Where else?"

"But—aren't funerals supposed to be at a church?"

"No, Beany. There are no rules. You can have a funeral wherever you want. Besides, we don't go to church. And even if we did, who'd show up, the three of us? I'm not wasting money on a church or a funeral home or whatever. Besides, Gus belongs in the river."

Claire writes something on the notepad.

"What do you mean, *he belongs in the river*?"

"It's what he wanted, Bean. To have his ashes scattered in the river. Your grandmother's ashes were scattered there too."

I lean against the kitchen counter and wipe my forehead. Maybe that was one of the reasons Gus went out on the river every day. To feel closer to my grandmother.

"Henry would've come," I say. "To the funeral. And so would Gus's friends."

"What friends?" my mom asks.

"He had friends!" I say, even though I'm not so sure.

My mom wipes her own forehead and takes a long drink from her coffee mug. "I'm handling this, Beany. It's all taken care of. It'll be just you, me, and Claire and a nice quiet ceremony at the river. The sooner we get this over with the better."

"What about Henry? And Sally? I want them there!"

"Sally? You mean Henry's mom? Honestly, Bean, she hasn't even left her house in years, has she? You think she's going to leave the house for some grumpy old man she never even met?"

Claire closes her notebook and looks up at me. She doesn't say anything, but I'm sure she's thinking my mom has a point. I hate her.

"They're coming," I say.

My mom looks up at me and I finally see some sympathy in her eyes. "I'm sorry. I know how much Gus meant to you. If you want to invite Henry and Sally, you can. Just don't get your hopes up about Sally."

"I will," I say. "And they'll come." I hope it's not a lie. I turn around, walk down the hallway, and go outside. It's early but already it's hot and humid. My feet move instinctively to Henry's.

The walk seems longer and slower than usual. When I was little, sometimes Gus would take me with him on his daily trip to the MiniMart. He'd hold my hand even though we were on the sidewalk. I remember the way his bony hands felt. How sometimes I could feel the bones under his wrinkly skin. We didn't talk much, but sometimes he'd nod at an empty house with a For Sale sign in front as we'd pass by and tell me a little story about the people who used to live there and where they'd gone.

"How come you never left?" I asked once.

He stopped walking and gently dropped my hand. He breathed in deeply, as if he were taking the whole neighborhood into his lungs.

"I couldn't leave," he said quietly. "This place is all I know. Where all my memories are." He'd looked at me with sad eyes, and I remember wishing there was more for him. More than just memories and always looking back.

As I walk the final steps to Henry's, I pause and look at the neighborhood behind me, realizing it's all I know, too. But it won't always be. Someday, I'll make it out.

I breathe in the way Gus did, almost tasting the hot air. Then I let it out, and knock on the door.

Henry is always the one to open it, but today Sally is there. She greets me by wrapping her arms around me and pulling me to her chest. She smells like rotten flower vase water. "Oh, Bean Girl," she says. "I am so sorry about your grampa."

It sounds odd to hear Gus referred to as Grampa. It feels odd to see Sally standing up.

"Come sit," she tells me.

I follow her to the couch. She's wearing her usual housedress that covers up all of her folds. She must not have put a fresh one on yet.

Good Morning America is on the TV.

"Henry's still sleeping. Do you want to sit and watch *GMA* for a while? There's Entenmann's on the kitchen counter you can help yourself to."

An empty plate rests on the coffee table. A few light streaks of raspberry jam and a lone crumb remain on the flowered plate. One streak looks like a fingerprint, and I try not to picture Sally scraping up the last bits with her fingers.

We watch *GMA* quietly until an ad comes on, then I turn to Sally. She smiles at me in her special way. When she smiles, it's not just her mouth but her whole face that changes.

"Sally," I say, "I know this is an awful lot to ask, but—"

I pause when our eyes meet. Sometimes, I think Sally can see through my chest and into my heart. When she looks at me like this, she feels more like a mom than my own ever has.

"What is it, Beany?"

I look down at my hands. "I was wondering if you

might come to Gus's funeral. It'll be just down the road, at the riverside. And just my mom and her friend Claire will be there. I know you don't like to leave the house much. But, I was hoping—"

Why am I crying?

"Oh, Bean," Sally says, pulling me toward her. I breathe through my mouth to avoid the dead flowers and cry harder.

"Beany Bean," Sally says. She runs her hand through my hair like normal moms do to their little kids when they're sad or hurt.

"I'm sorry, Sally. Never mind. It's just that my mom is acting so weird. She doesn't care that Gus is dead at all. I swear. I just wish someone could be there who cares. I mean, I know you didn't know Gus, but—" I picture Claire and my mom talking about Gus at the table, and hear their horrible giggles. "At least you have a heart."

Sally leans back and sighs.

I should never have asked for something so big.

At the end of the hall, Henry's door opens. He walks out in a sleep-induced stupor. He's wearing plaid boxers that go to his knees and a T-shirt that falls well below his waist. Henry isn't really *that* chubby. Just a little soft-looking in spots. But he always wears baggy clothes to hide himself in. Instead of coming out to see us, he goes into the bathroom. His electric toothbrush hums for what is most likely precisely two minutes. Sally and I watch a chef on *GMA* stand outside, sweating like mad as he makes barbecue chicken for the camera, and the predictable fans make faces behind his back.

After Henry eats, showers, and gets dressed, and I have watched way too much *GMA*, we leave the house and walk down to the MiniMart to get Sally a new box of Entenmann's and us some TV relief.

"You'll come to the funeral, right?" I ask Henry.

"Of course," he says, shuffling along beside me and pulling at his shirt. When we get to the store, we buy our usual stuff, then sit on the empty bike rack and go halvsies on candy choices, just like always. We start with our melting Twix and finish with Skittles. Henry studies the nutrition label on the Twix wrapper and frowns. "We should really switch to peppermint patties," he says. It says right on the wrapper '70 percent less fat than the average of the leading chocolate brands.'"

I roll my eyes. "Half a candy bar is not going to make you explode."

While Henry quietly chews his share of Skittles, I imagine Claire and my mom back at home, making whatever excuse for plans they need to make. If it wasn't so hot, I would stay right here with Henry all day. But a drip of sweat trickles down his cheek. He quickly wipes it away and stands up, then reaches his hand out to help pull me up, too. We walk back to his house in silence.

When we get there, we stop at the end of the driveway.

"You want to stay here?" he asks.

"Yes. But I think I should go home."

Henry nods. "Okay. I'll see you at the funeral," he says. "But, Bean . . . don't count on Sally. I mean . . . you know."

"Yeah," I say. "I know."

He nods again. "Well, I'll see ya." The plastic MiniMart bag rustles against his leg as he walks up the driveway and disappears into the house.

chapter five

On the morning of Gus's funeral, I'm cursing my too-tight sandals when the front doorbell rings. My mom yells for me to see who it is.

When I get to the door, Sally is standing on the other side of the screen next to Henry. She's holding a bouquet of flowers. I bet they're from the MiniMart. The ones that are prewrapped in clear plastic that sit in white buckets filled with murky water near the checkout.

I do not let my jaw drop when I see her. Instead, I let my heart grow with gratitude, and try to show it to her in my smile. I open the door and take the flowers and invite them in. Sally gives me a long, silent hug. She squeezes me so tightly, I feel empty when she lets go. I take Sally and Henry to the living room, and we sit on the couch while we wait for my mom and Claire to finish getting ready. Every so often, Sally sighs and pats my knee. I want to tell her how grateful I am that she's here. But I think that might embarrass her, to point out what a huge step it was just to leave her house. So I stay quiet and thank her in my head.

When it's time to go, we walk in our pathetic procession. First my mom, then Claire, then me, Henry, and Sally. Sally is several paces behind, squinting hard as she trudges along behind us in the bright sun. I wonder what it must feel like to her, to have the sun shine on her for the first time in so long. Like a bear must feel coming out of hibernation. Henry and I keep turning back to make sure she's still there.

When we get to the riverbank, we form a half circle, looking out over the smelly river Gus fished in every day. My mom clears her throat and shifts the heavy-looking dark blue cardboard box in her arms that she's lugged all the way. Her hands on the box look small but strong. Her fingers curl over the edges in a sure grip.

"Beany," she says, holding the box just inches from her chest like an offering she can't hand over, "why don't you say a few words?"

"What?" I don't know what I expected to happen at this sorry attempt at a funeral, but it didn't involve me doing any talking.

The others all watch me expectantly, as if I am going to say something profound and meaningful like they do on the soap funerals. I rack my brain for some memory of a recent death played out on *Days*.

"Um—" I start. I breathe in slowly, trying to think of what to say to their expectant ears.

My eyes rest on Sally in her large, tentlike flowing dress covered with pink and peach flowers. I could probably count on one hand the number of times I've seen Sally standing up in the eight years I've known her. I wonder how she got the dress and imagine her bidding for it on eBay, or ordering it through some plus-size catalog, though I've never seen any catalogs in their house. All I've ever seen there are *TV Guide*s and *Soap Opera Digest*s. Maybe Henry had to go online with her and help her pick something out. And then she probably had to pay tons extra to have it shipped overnight. Or maybe she's had it all along, for the day she's imagined—when Henry's dad comes back. In Sally's soap world, anyone can return, even from the dead.

She nods at me with her gentle, mascaraed eyes and smiles encouragingly.

I clear my throat. "Gus—" I begin, then pause.

My mom shifts her weight impatiently from foot to foot, and Claire bites the inside of her mouth.

"Gus was a good grandfather," I say.

I catch my mom giving Claire a doubtful look.

"He loved to fish," I continue, glancing over at the river. I try to imagine him there in happier days. "He loved his wife," I add.

What else did he love? What else? Were there only two things?

"He loved this river," I say, gesturing toward the murky water. "He always hoped one day they would clean it up. And—" Across the water on the other bank a car drives by, blasting hip-hop. The bass carries all the way over to our side, practically rattling my teeth.

Henry sniffs and fans his sports jacket. There is no way with his getup he'll be avoiding sweat spots today.

Sally nods at me again to keep going as soon as the music fades down the street.

My mom sighs impatiently, like she hadn't intended me to take so long and now she wants me to wrap it up.

"I loved him," I blurt out. I can almost see the unfamiliar words hovering in the air. I never told him that. I've never told *anyone* that.

I look at the box in my mom's arms. "I did," I say to it. I want to take the box and hug it to my heart. Saying those words out loud makes me realize how true they are. I don't want to let go of him now that I know what's real. I feel my arms slowly start to reach toward the box.

"He loved you, too," my mom says quietly. Before I can touch the box, she turns and looks out at the river where she'll let him go.

Sally wipes her eyes with an already very soggy tissue. She always cries during soap funerals.

My arms drop back to my sides. "May he rest in peace," I say, finally remembering a familiar funeral phrase. It sounds much better than good-bye.

"May he rest in peace," Sally repeats. Claire, Henry, and my mom echo Sally, but not all at the same time so it sounds mumbled and awkward.

"Okay," my mom says. "I guess it's time."

She carries the box closer to the edge of the bank. We follow, keeping a few steps back. She fumbles with the lid.

"Let me—" Claire starts to say. But my mom shakes her off and manages to get it open herself.

Inside, there's a large plastic bag, which she somehow unseals, then she steps closer to the edge of the embankment. She doesn't look back as we inch up behind her. The box seems heavy as she struggles to hold it out over the water, then turns it upside down. Almost at once, heavy-looking gray ash slowly flows out of the box just as a gust of wind blows off the water, spraying the ashes against our legs.

Sally shrieks.

"Oh, shit," Claire says.

The grit settles between my toes in my new sandals. I can't bear to look.

Sally glances down at her swollen ankles. Dark ashes cling to her sheer, coral-colored nylons. She does a little jig sort of thing to get the ashes to fall off without having to brush them off with her bare hands, but it doesn't help.

Henry stares at his once-shiny black shoes, now covered with a layer of dust.

"Jesus," my mom says. She looks down at her own ash-covered toes. Her body goes a bit limp. I think it's the first time since she cried on the kitchen floor that she looks remotely emotional over the loss of Gus. Slowly, she lifts her face to the sky and holds out her arms, dropping the empty blue box.

"Happy now?" she asks the sole cloud in the sky. I'm not sure if she's talking to Gus or God.

We all stand there, waiting for something to happen.

The grit between my toes chafes and I wiggle them just a bit to try to set it free. There's a larger, sharper piece under my big toe. I pray it isn't bone. But what else could it be?

I catch Claire watching me try to rid my feet of the stuff and stop.

No one says a word. We all just stand there with Gus's dust clinging to us. I look down at the empty box, then up at my mom. She sighs and blinks her eyes up at the sky, as if she is silently asking someone up there what we're supposed to do now. We all follow her gaze. Waiting.

Then my mom's shoulders start to shake and she laughs out loud. Claire looks at her nervously. Maybe even a little disapprovingly. But my mom just cracks up. She kicks off her sandals and howls. And then Claire is laughing, too. The two of them hold on to each other, cackling like this is the funniest thing they've ever seen.

As Henry, Sally, and I watch the two of them, I try not to think about the gray, gritty dust still clinging to my sweaty feet inside my sandals. I concentrate on putting all my energy into hating my mom and Claire. But pretty soon, I can't stand it anymore. I bend down and undo my sandal straps so I can try to wipe off the ash in the dusty, dry grass.

Following my lead, Henry bends down and gently sweeps the ash off his new shoes. Only Sally doesn't budge.

She just watches, horror-struck by my mom and Claire's behavior.

"Come on, Sally," my mom says. "We're not all that bad. The old grump's probably looking down at us and having a good laugh. If he actually made it up there," she adds.

I squint up at the lone cloud and think for sure if Gus could see us he would *not* be laughing. He would be shaking his head, bitterly disappointed in my mom yet again.

My mom walks over to Sally and tries to brush the rest of the ash from Sally's elephantlike ankles.

Henry looks mortified.

Grandpa, I'm sorry, I say in my head. I know it's too late to call him that now. But the word seems so much warmer than *Gus*. There's love in that word.

Claire picks up the empty box from the ground and tucks it under her arm. With her free hand, she laces her fingers through my mom's and leads her back toward the house.

Sally follows several feet behind, moving carefully. Her soggy pink tissue hangs limply from her hand. She doesn't look back or wait for us.

"Well, that was interesting," Henry says when the others are far enough ahead to be out of earshot.

"That's my mom," I say. "Interesting."

But she's more than that. At the moment, I think she's worse than that. But I don't say so. I try to gather some of the ashes on the ground into a pile and scoop them up in my hands. Henry bends down to help.

"We'll never get it all," I say.

Henry tries to scoop up some of what I've missed, but it's no use. We walk to the edge of the bank and throw the ash out as far as we can. But there's still grit on our hands, and in the grass.

"How could my mom laugh?" I ask. "How could she think this was funny?"

Henry doesn't answer for a while. Instead he looks out at the water. Bits of trash float past us in the current.

"To a stranger, the scene might have looked faintly amusing," he says. "You have to admit it."

"It wasn't a *scene*, it was real!"

I try to imagine some other family holding a service for their loved one on this sorry excuse for a riverbank. Gus said it used to be beautiful here, back when it was still a thriving mill town and the old Victorian houses that line our street were called Painted Ladies, and people sat on their porches and took romantic rowboat rides along the river, and you could still eat the fish.

"It wasn't amusing," I say. "Pathetic is more like it."

I turn to face the water again, hoping at least some of Gus's ashes made it down to the current and then, who knows where. I imagine that part of him gliding with the current and eventually finding his way to the ocean, to freedom, away from this place.

"Come on," Henry says. "Let's get back." He reaches for my hand. It feels familiar in mine even though I don't think I've ever held it. As we start toward the house, I turn one more time and, with my free hand, wave good-bye.

chapter six

When we reach the house, Henry's hand slips out of mine. I feel cold, even though it's baking hot outside. I feel like I might float away without Henry hanging on to me.

But I don't. I just stand here with the tall, paint-peeling house standing over us. Finally, I lead Henry to the back of the house so we can rinse our hands at the spigot Gus used for gardening. As we approach, we see a giant pair of coral nylons hanging alone on the clothesline that never gets used. The large legs hang limply in the windless air, like two recently shed snake skins. I can almost feel Henry cringe. We both turn away and rinse our hands in the cold water. I avoid looking at the puddle we've made on the ground under the spigot, and try not to think that a little of Gus is in it.

"Come on," Henry says when we've rubbed our hands almost raw. He leads the way back to the front of the house.

I follow him inside. Busy cooking sounds waft from the kitchen. Sally and Claire are sitting at the kitchen table with what look like Bloody Marys, celery stalks and all. They both have cutting boards in front of them. Claire chops onions while Sally attempts to dice tomatoes. Sally's meals usually come out of a box or a can, and it's clear she's not too sure about how to use the knife.

My mom is busy rushing back and forth from the stove to the kitchen table to the sink to the refrigerator. I look at Henry as he takes in the scene, too. He raises his eyebrows and I know exactly what he is thinking: *Welcome to Bizarro World.*

Sally looks up at us with an expression I've never seen her use. I can't tell if she is nervously happy or terrified.

It's not clear what my mom's making, but all four burners on the stove are in use, and the oven has two casserole dishes inside. It feels like Thanksgiving without the football. And without Gus.

When my mom finally notices Henry and me, she says, "Good," and marches over to the fridge. She pulls out a giant container of the sauce she made that day and puts it on the counter. Then she goes over to the stove, grabs the biggest pot, and carries it to the sink. Lasagna noodles slap loudly into the strainer as she tips the giant pot.

"Come here and do the building, you two," she says.

I open my mouth to remind her that I'm not supposed to know how to cook, but before I can, Henry walks over and peers into the empty dish as if sizing it up. My mom opens the oven and pulls out a huge casserole dish filled with roasted vegetables. They're still sizzling when she places the dish on a pad on the counter in front of Henry.

"Oh, crap. I forgot the ricotta. Okay. Beany, you do it." She grabs a bunch of stuff from the fridge and puts it in front of me with an empty bowl.

"I don't know how," I lie.

The truth is, I've always wanted to learn how to cook like my grandmother, even if my mom forbade it. All these years of sitting at the kitchen table while my mom cooked for Gus and me, I couldn't help but learn, even if my fingers never did the actual construction.

My mom ignores my lie and leaves me to it.

I scoop the ricotta out of the bucket and dump the soft white stuff into the bowl. Then I cut the fresh mozzarella into small chunks and drop them in, too.

"You need basil, don't forget," my mom says behind me. She drops a handful of chopped green leaves into the mixture.

I grate some Parmesan onto the top of the heap, add salt, pepper, and nutmeg, and stir it all together. Henry watches me with a look of admiration. It feels good.

The kitchen is hot and steamy and smells like an Italian restaurant. My mom always said her dream was to have her own place, making food instead of serving it. She even designed a menu with all my grandmother's Italian dishes she planned to serve. She drew delicate grapevines between the courses. The sketches were beautiful, and I remember Gus muttering something about wasted talent. It was his way of complimenting her, even though it was also a jab. Sometimes when my mom made a dish my grandmother taught her, Gus would say, "Tastes just like Stella's—" and then he'd get a sad look on his face and leave the room.

The restaurant was the only thing Gus shared with my mom—dreams beyond her working at Lou's. He'd buy the Powerball ticket every Tuesday and wait, clutching the thing, comparing numbers when they read them off during the break in the nightly news. And I would think, *Don't you see that, Mom? He wants something for you. He's not the horrible father you think he is.* But then I would remember the way he spoke to her and just feel all confused. How could you love and hate someone at the same time?

"One more layer," my mom says, leaning over my shoulder. Henry looks at me doubtfully. There is no way one more layer is going to fit in that pan. We fake it, moving our hands through the various steps while my mom makes herself busy at the sink.

"Let us help you, Lexie," Claire says. She and Sally have finished chopping and cleaned the table off, save for their Bloody Marys, which are now nearly empty. I've never seen Sally drink before. Her cheeks are pink and glisten with sweat.

My mom ignores Claire's offer and begins washing dishes like a maniac.

"Done," I say, sprinkling the last of the mozzarella over the final layer.

"Oven." My mom wipes her hands on her apron, walks over to the kitchen table, and drops into the chair between Sally and Claire.

"I need a drink," she says.

Claire stands up to make one and stumbles slightly.

I put the lasagna in the oven, then wash my hands and go back into the living room, waiting for Henry to follow. A minute later he comes in with a bottle of Gus's five-dollar table wine under his arm. I have no idea how he managed to sneak it out, but Henry moves in a quiet way. Sometimes you can forget he's in a room with you.

"Nice move," I tell him.

He nods and pulls Gus's corkscrew out of his pants pocket.

I manage to open the bottle and realize the one thing Henry forgot was glasses. I bring the bottle to my lips and take a small sip, then pass it to Henry. He makes a face.

"It's an acquired taste," I say.

"Understatement," he says, after forcing himself to swallow.

We share back and forth until my mom calls us from the kitchen to say dinner is ready. She hustles us all into the dining room. Besides lasagna, she's made some sort of squash casserole, herbed potatoes, salad, and focaccia.

While Claire lights the candles in the candelabra, Sally

42

waddles over to the seat at the head of the table, farthest from the kitchen. Gus's seat. But she couldn't know that. My mom takes the seat at the opposite end and Henry, Claire, and I fill the middle.

No one seems to notice that Henry's cheeks are fiery red. I touch my own hot face and try to cool my cheeks with my hands.

When we're all settled at our seats, my mom goes back to the kitchen and returns with two bottles of Gus's favorite wine that he saves for special occasions. It's from Montepulciano, where his family came from. He always had a bottle on his and my grandmother's anniversary. He'd say a toast to her, and my mom would look uncomfortable. Then we'd all take a drink—me from a glass that only had about a sip's worth.

My mom opens the bottle like a pro. Being a waitress, she's probably opened a thousand bottles at least. She makes her way around the table, filling our glasses equally. When she's done, we raise our glasses after her. Rich food aromas circle the table, mixing with the smell of the melting wax of the candles. I feel dizzy.

"To Gus," she says loudly. She looks at his chair, occupied by Sally, and I swear—just at that moment—something in her expression shows that she misses him.

"To Gus," we repeat. And we all take a sip.

The taste brings me right back to all those October twenty-firsts, sitting at this table with Gus and my mom, listening to him tell us year after year about how he and my grandmother met, about their honeymoon in Italy and how he'd always promised to take my grandmother back again someday, but he never got the chance. My mom catches my eye as she puts her glass down, and I wonder if she's having the same memory, feeling the same regret. Right at that moment, I promise Gus that I will always drink this wine on their anniversary, and someday, someday I will go to Montepulciano for the two of them.

After the toast, we eat quietly. Claire and my mom keep exchanging looks and smiling at each other with the more wine they drink. I bite my lip to keep from telling my mom to stop acting so happy. Sally seems uncomfortable at the end of the table. I wonder how long it's been since she had dinner with anyone besides Henry and me at her house, sitting on the scratchy plaid sofa watching *E! News*.

Throughout dinner, my mom keeps getting up to refill Claire and Sally's glasses, And her own, of course.

"Oh, Sally," she slurs, between not-so-elegant sips. "I can't believe you've lived on the same street as us all this time and I've never met you before! Never seen you! We should've gotten together years ago!"

"Well," Sally says quietly, looking down at her plate, "I don't really get out all that much."

I don't think Sally has left the house since Henry's dad disappeared. That's when Sally closed the doors to the outside forever. Until today. Sally collects some kind of disability money and paid for the house outright with money she inherited from Henry's grandparents. But this isn't really the kind of information you share with new friends.

When we finish eating, Henry and I escape back to the living room with our wineglasses. My mom insists that she will do all the cleaning up as long as Sally and Claire keep her company in the kitchen. I know what this means. After-dinner drinks.

Henry and I sit on the couch with our feet propped up on the coffee table, our glasses resting on our full bellies. The faded gold wallpaper on the wall behind Gus's chair starts to rise and fall, and I feel like I might throw up.

Henry doesn't look too good, either.

Gus's empty chair glares at us as we listen to our moms and Claire get more and more drunk. Their chatty voices gradually turn to high-pitched giggles. Henry keeps glancing toward the door with a worried expression on his face.

Then Sally snorts. There's no mistake it's her. Henry winces.

"Let's get some fresh air," I say, fumbling a little as I stand.

"Definitely."

"Where are we going?" he asks when we get outside.

"Let's go out on the water. Let's take Gus's boat."

"We're too drunk."

"Screw that," I say. I don't sound like me at all. I don't sound like I want to sound. I want us to be quiet together. I just want peace.

Henry rolls his eyes. "No. We'll go tomorrow."

I cross my arms like a baby not getting my way and stumble.

"You okay?"

My stomach convulses. "Oh, God!" I run to the bushes just in time. Everything comes hurling out of me. Everything. The wine and the food and all those horrible flavors of the day. Everything emptying out.

I feel Henry behind me.

"Go away," I say.

Another wave pushes up and I let it come out in an embarrassingly loud heave.

Henry's fingers gently pull my hair away from my face as he stands close behind me. I reach up and feel his puffy hand on my cheek. He slips it out from under mine and puts it on my forehead, as if I'm a little kid and he's checking to see if I have a fever.

I don't know why it feels so good. I don't know why it makes me cry.

We stand there until I'm sure I'm done, then Henry walks me back inside. Our moms are still in the kitchen talking way too loudly.

"I'll go get her and walk her home," Henry says. He doesn't look too excited about having to do it, and I don't blame him. But I know it's something I can't exactly help with, so I nod.

"Thanks for everything today, Hen." I put my hand on his arm. It's a little sticky from sweat. I think he's blushing but it's hard to tell in the dim light of the entryway.

"Go get some sleep," he says. He turns away from me and walks slowly toward the kitchen, as if he's dreading what he'll find.

"Henry!" My mom's drunken voice booms from the doorway.

I cringe and, like a coward, go upstairs by myself.

chapter seven

When I wake up, the house is quiet. I try to lift my head, but it hurts too much. I watch the crack in my ceiling and listen to the nothingness. Pretty soon, I notice the birds singing outside my window. The morning traffic. A siren in the distance. Someone's dog barking. All the life-moving-forward noises I never paid attention to before. Gus's death doesn't matter to anyone outside my window. Maybe even outside my bedroom door.

In the hallway, his bedroom door is closed again. I open it. The room feels still and calm and unmoving, like one of those fake rooms in a museum where you're supposed to marvel at how well-preserved the contents are. I place the framed photo I took earlier back on the antique dresser where it belongs and sit on the edge of the old four-poster bed. I run my fingers along the soft fabric of the bedspread, making a wrinkle trail. If it was up to me, I would keep the room just like this forever. It's the only room in the house where you can sense love existed.

I look at my grandparents' happy faces. Forever smiling in here. I wish I could feel what they felt.

Downstairs, the ticks of the grandfather clock in the entryway sound louder than usual. *Hel-lo, hel-lo, hel-lo,* they seem to say in a mocking way.

When I pass the living room, I glance at Gus's chair and wonder if my mom will get rid of it. She's always hated it, how old and dented and so clearly his it is. I can tell by the way she looks at it with disgust, whenever he isn't—wasn't—in the room.

I hate how much she hated him. And I hate that he helped feed it.

Just a couple of weeks ago, my mom was late coming home again. Gus was waiting up for her, and, secretly, so was I.

"Where've you been?" he whispered loudly when she finally stumbled up the stairs. He was standing in his bedroom doorway, which she had to pass to get to her room. My lights were off but my door was open so I could see into the hall. My mom stood in the hallway wearing a short skirt and high heels.

"Out," she whispered back, glancing toward my door.

"Dressed like that?" Gus asked. "Why dressed like that?"

Their whispers sounded like hisses.

"Like what, Dad?" she asked.

"Like *that*. Like trash."

I cringed and watched my mom do the same. I hated knowing Gus could be cruel.

"You're asking for it dressed like that," he said. "Asking for it all over again."

"Trash, huh? You don't know shit," my mom said.

There was a smack, followed by a brief quiet, and then my mom's hurried footsteps. Her door slammed. Then Gus's door clicked shut. I could feel the disappointment in that click. But the echo of the slap was there, too. And that was so much worse.

I crept into the hall and waited for the light under his door to go out. Then I went to my mom's room. I lay down on the floor in the hallway and put my ear to the crack under her door.

"I hate him," she sobbed. She was on the phone. "Claire. I hate him. Maybe you're right. Maybe I should just tell him the truth."

Memories of the big secret I'd overheard when I was twelve made my heart start to race.

"But if he kicks me out—" There was a long pause, except for my mom's sniffing. "No. I can't do it. I know what it's like to lose your mother. I can't do that to her." Another pause. Crying. "Damn it, Claire. I'm trapped. I've been trapped my whole life."

It got quiet again. I put my hand on my chest to try to stop my heart from beating so hard.

"It's just so complicated. He's so good with her. Better

50

than I am, that's for sure. She needs him. Maybe when she's a little older—just a minute."

I held my breath as her bed creaked and her footsteps started for the door, then stopped.

"Sorry, I thought I heard something. Oh, what would I do without you? I don't know how I'd survive it all."

Her heavy words pushed me away from her door. I got up and leaned against the wall. There was a pause, then she started giggling. I picked myself up and crept back to my room before she got off the phone.

Back in my own bed, I imagined what things would be like if I was never born. It was a game I played a lot. And always, what I imagined was a better life for my mom. And Gus.

That was only a few weeks ago, but it feels like one more piece I can't quite fit into the rest of the puzzle that is our life.

In the kitchen, I open the freezer and take out the coffee beans and the bag of mini Snickers my mom keeps hidden under two packages of frozen peas. I grind the beans extra long just to wake up my mom. While the coffee's brewing, I eat a Snickers whole and let the chocolate coating melt between my tongue and the roof of my mouth.

"I see you," a voice says behind me.

I jump about a mile.

Claire.

What's she *doing* here? Probably she was too drunk to drive home. Again.

"Morning," I say through my stuffed mouth.

Claire gets two mugs out of the cabinet and stands by the coffeemaker. I never noticed how truly skinny she is. And pointy. Pointy elbows, pointy fingers, pointy nose, and chin. Even her jawline is pointy.

I wait for the Snickers to defrost enough so I can chew and swallow.

"I didn't know you stayed over again," I say.

"Your mom needs me."

Why?

I don't know what I ever did, but Claire has never seemed to like me. The few times I've spent with her when my mom invited me to go to the movies with them or, on the rare occasion, out to dinner, I always got the feeling Claire didn't want me there. Like they couldn't gossip about all the things they wanted to with me around.

"What are you doing today?" she asks, making small talk. I'm sure she's forcing herself to smile.

"I'm going fishing with Henry," I tell her. "In Gus's boat."

She stops smiling and scrunches her pointy nose. "In that river? Are you high?"

"Gus did it, why can't we?"

"Because you are sane. At least I thought so. And Gus was a crazy old geezer."

"Don't say that." I really want to hit her.

She raises her eyebrows at me, like she's surprised I'm standing up for him. "Sorry," she says. "But are you sure that's a safe thing to do? Seriously, Bean. That water is, like, toxic."

"I've been out there before. Gus used to take me."

She shrugs, like it's not really that important whether I get exposed to toxic river water after all. "Suit yourself then," she says.

She pulls the coffeepot from the machine, even though it's still dripping a little. The drips sizzle on the burner while she pours two cups. I start to hold out my hand, thinking one's for me, but she walks past me and goes back toward the stairs in the hall.

"Thanks a lot," I say under my breath.

I pour my own cup and grab another Snickers. I sit at the kitchen table and dip the Snickers in the coffee and suck off the melted chocolate. My head hurts a little less, but not much. Even from the kitchen I can still hear the grandfather clock ticking, only with a different message. *Get-out, get-out, get-out.*

The doorbell rings before I finish my third Snickers and an inch of my coffee. Only Henry rings the doorbell.

"Enter!" I call.

The screen door whines open and clicks shut. I count his soft steps coming toward me. Just once I would like to hear Henry make some noise.

"Ouch," I say when he comes into the kitchen. He looks even worse than I feel.

"What do you do for a hangover?" he asks.

"I don't know," I tell him. "My mom always says 'hair of the dog' and drinks a Bloody Mary. But I don't know how to make one."

"Me either. Maybe we could try straight tomato juice?"

"Yuck. Just the smell of that stuff makes me want to puke."

"What then?" He looks desperate.

"Coffee and chocolate seem to be helping a little." I pour him a cup and get him the whole bag. We eat and drink, staring at the tabletop. Soon, in addition to feeling hungry, I feel completely hyper and shaky.

"I still feel awful," I say.

"Me too. Maybe we need fresh air."

A high-pitched giggle escapes from upstairs.

"Ugh. Let's get out of here."

We leave the empty Snickers bag and our dirty mugs on the table and make our way outside.

It's still pretty early but already unbearably hot when we step onto the front porch. Henry and I squint toward the old carriage house Gus used as a garage.

"Come on," I say.

When we step inside, we see Gus's old Chevy sitting there, waiting to be taken for its daily drive down to the MiniMart for the paper and coffee. Gus always said he wasn't social, but I never believed him entirely. He could have had the paper delivered, and he definitely could have drunk the coffee my mom made every morning. The only thing he couldn't get at home was the scratch ticket he bought every day. And possibly a friendly smile from whoever was working behind the counter—which was a lot more than he got at home if I'd already left for school.

"Where's the fishing pole?" Henry asks.

I gesture toward the far wall, neatly lined with hooks that have things dangling from them: paint brushes, hammers, tools I don't know the names of, and Gus's old green fishing rod. My small orange pole is hanging there, too, covered with dust and attached to a series of deserted cobwebs.

"Let's go!" Henry says cheerfully, grabbing both poles.

"Um. We need bait," I say.

Henry looks confused. Poor Henry. He never had someone to take him fishing.

"Oh, you mean from the tackle box!" he says excitedly. He scans the workbench and opens Gus's gray metal toolbox, then shuts it quickly when he realizes his mistake.

"Where is it?"

"The red plastic box," I say. "Right here." I reach under the bench where Gus always kept the box and drag it out.

Inside, there are several hooks and flies, some fake bugs and fish, and an old photo of my grandmother taped inside the lid covered with plastic wrap to keep it dry. It's a black-and-white photo of her in her wedding gown. She looks happy and beautiful. I've never seen the photograph before. I don't remember it from when Gus took me fishing. I wonder when he decided to start bringing her with him.

An ache grows in my chest as I imagine Gus carefully taping the photo in his box and peeking at my grandmother when they were out on the river. Did he talk to her? Did he tell her how sad and lonely he was? How much he missed her?

"Ooh, cool!" Henry says, peering over my shoulder at the lures.

"Oh, shoot. I don't know how to use any of these," I say. "Gus always tied them for me. You're going to have to dig for some worms."

"Worms?"

"Well, you'll have to put *something* on the hook. It's not like the fish swim up to the hook and think, 'Yeah, okay. I'll just stick this pointy metal thing through my jaw.'"

Henry rolls his eyes. "Just tell me how I get a worm."

I grab an old tomato soup can from a small stack under the workbench and reach for a trowel hanging from a hook on the wall.

"Take these, go in the garden, and dig a hole. You'll find one in no time."

He takes the can and trowel carefully, as if he doesn't want to get his hands dirty. As he steps out of the dusty garage and into the sun, he pauses to see if I'm going to follow, but I stay behind and study the photo of my grandmother. I wonder how different things would be if she hadn't died when my mom was so young. Maybe my mom wouldn't have gotten pregnant. Maybe I would never have been born. Maybe my mom and grandfather wouldn't have hated each other.

You and me, I think, looking at the photo. *We really screwed things up.*

"I got one!" Henry yells from the garden.

I carefully close the lid with the photograph and carry the tackle box and pole outside, leaving my old pole leaning against the bench.

Henry runs over to me holding out the can. I peek inside and see one lowly worm squirming in a pathetic sprinkle of soil.

"I think we're gonna need more than one," I say.

He frowns and turns back for the garden. This time, I follow.

The tomato plants Gus put in at the end of May are starting to flower. I wonder if my mom will bother to take care of them. I wish I could remember what to do. Gus used to let me follow him up and down the few tiny rows, pointing out which things were weeds and letting me pull them out. Whenever we found a worm or some other bug, Gus would tell me what its job was. If it was bad for the garden, he'd gather it in his hand and plop it in a coffee can. Then he'd take the thing out behind the carriage house and leave it. I never saw him kill a single creature.

I wish my mom knew that about him. That sometimes, he could be gentle. I wish just once he could have been that way with her.

"I got another one!" Henry says excitedly.

"Let's go then," I say.

He nods and sidles up beside me, holding the can out in front of him proudly.

"What?" he asks when he catches me smiling at him.

"Oh . . . nothing."

He peers excitedly into the can to check on the worms.

I try to remember the last time I felt like Henry looks, and come up empty.

chapter eight

At the end of the street there's a path that leads down to a small dock where a few boats are locked up. The key to Gus's lock is in the tackle box. The keychain is a red-and-white foam buoy with a single key. Gus left the oars and life preservers in the bottom of the boat. So far, no one has ever stolen them, which is pretty surprising for our neighborhood.

I hold the bow while Henry steps into the rowboat. It tips sharply to one side and Henry lets out a yelp.

"Relax!" I say. "Just get in the middle and make your way to the seat in the bow." I point so he knows where that is.

I get in after him and put the oars in the locks. "Shove off!" I say.

Henry looks at me, confused.

"Put your hand on the dock and push," I explain.

He gives us a gentle shove and we slowly drift out on

the stinky river. It smells like the city when it rains in the summer. Like rotting garbage. When I dip the paddles in the water, they make a soft, familiar splash.

"How come you never took me out here before?" Henry asks.

I turn back to face him as he looks across the water to the overgrown riverbank. A lone, discarded stove pokes out of the high grass. A seagull sits on a tire, watching us curiously.

"Why would anyone want to come out here?" I ask. "It's disgusting."

He shrugs. "Gus liked it."

"Yeah, well. Some people think Gus was crazy." I remember Claire's cold words and cringe a little.

"Not you, though," Henry says.

I eye the red tackle box at my feet and picture the photo of my grandmother inside. "You gonna fish, or what?" I ask. I pull in the oars so we can drift, the way Gus used to do when we fished together. I turn myself around so I can sit facing Henry.

He grins and reaches for the pole. He fumbles with the hook and then reaches into the soup can wedged between his white sneakers.

"Ew," he says, holding the worm with two fingers.

"It won't bite you."

"I know, but . . . it's gross."

"Didn't you touch the worm when you dug it up?"

He wrinkles his nose. "I used the little shovel thing."

"You mean the trowel, Henry. Jeez."

He shrugs and gently tries to wrap the long worm around the hook.

"You're supposed to spear the hook *through* the worm, ya know," I say.

"I'm not stupid. I just can't do it."

"Why not?"

"It's mean."

"And submerging the thing underwater so it can be eaten by a giant, pollution-filled fish is an act of charity?"

He shrugs again and inspects the worm knot he's made around the hook. Then he lets the little worm dangle behind him on the line before he casts out and lets it sink into the tea-colored water. I'm surprised he knows how to cast and wonder where he picked that up. Probably on TV.

The small bobber on the line floats quietly on the top of the water.

"So, um, how long does this usually take?" Henry asks, peering at the water.

I shake my head at him. What would Gus think?

"Be patient," I say, closing my eyes and holding my face to the sun. "The whole point is to sit quietly and enjoy the peace.

He wrinkles his nose. "But not the smell."

"No, not the smell."

Less than a minute has gone by when the little bobber jerks. Henry practically falls out of the boat with excitement.

"I got one! I got one!" he yells.

"Pull it in!"

"How?"

"With the reel!"

He starts to crank the reel. The pole bends in a familiar arc. We both search the water to see what he's pulled up, but before the image of a struggling fish emerges, I suddenly don't want to see.

I turn away and squeeze my eyes shut.

"It's a fish!" Henry shouts, as if he was expecting an old tennis shoe.

"Let it loose!" I yell, not looking.

"What?"

"Let it go!" My chest tightens with panic. I cannot see the fish. I can't.

"But I don't know how!" Henry yells at me, his own panic sounding in his voice.

I'm crying.

"Hold its body with one hand and pull the hook out with the other," I say without looking. "You've got a barbless hook. Just do it!"

"Ick! It's slimy."

"Please, Henry. Just let it go!"

"I'm trying! Ew! Okay. Okay. I got it."

There's a splash.

"You can look now."

But I keep my hands over my face. I don't want him to see me crying. I'm not even sure why I'm crying in the first place.

"Beany? You okay?"

I wipe my face before I turn back and nod.

"I'm sorry. I just didn't want it to die."

"I wasn't going to kill it. I was going to let it go. I just wanted to see what it was like, you know? I never caught a fish before. It's one of the things you're supposed to do with your dad. It's on my list."

I look up in time to see him blush. "What list?"

"Never mind."

"No, tell me."

"It's dumb. It's something I started when I was little."

I sit forward. "This is me, Hen. Nothing you do is dumb to me. Well, almost nothing."

He sighs. "I made this list of all the things I would do with my dad. You know, if I had one. It's stupid."

I wipe my eyes again and look at the quiet, mucky water.

"I don't think it's stupid at all."

A clear lid with a chewed-up straw stuck through the star-shaped hole in the middle floats swiftly by among tiny flecks of dirt and debris. I wonder if ashes float or if they sink to the bottom of the river. Would they be mistaken for fish food? Or would they dissolve into the water and flow away from here into some cooler, cleaner place?

"Do you believe in heaven?" I ask.

There are almost no clouds in the sky. Just little wisps here and there.

"Nah," Henry says, looking up to where I'm gazing.

"Then what do you think happens when you die?"

He peers down into the worm can. "I dunno, Bean." He sounds sad. "What do you think?"

"I don't know, either. I mean, I can't imagine my mind just stopping. How can you turn into nothing? Like, where is Gus's mind right now? Does everything just stop? How can it just . . . stop?"

"I don't like thinking about it. If you think about that stuff too much, you start to go crazy."

"I know," I say. "But I can't help it."

We float along quietly, listening to distant car horns, brakes squeaking and engines revving as they make their way through the series of traffic lights down the busy road that parallels our quiet side street that runs along the river.

"Maybe . . . maybe it's kind of like not being born," Henry finally says.

"What do you mean?"

"Well, I don't know. I mean, do you remember before you were born?"

"No, of course not." I feel a twinge in my chest, thinking about my "what if I'd never been born" game.

"Well, maybe that's what it's like when you die, too."

He looks down at the water as if there will be some sort of confirmation to his theory just below the surface. I look down, too, wondering why not being able to see more than a foot below the surface makes it so interesting. Every so often we glide past more trash—soggy McDonald's fries containers getting ready to sink to the muddy bottom.

Fresh cigarette butts. The occasional empty soda bottle bobbing along.

"I hope it's not like that," I say. "God, it's like turning a switch. On, then off. That's it."

"But it wouldn't matter," he says. "Because you'd be gone."

I shake my head. "Let's go home."

The sun beats down on my back as I row. Henry twists forward so he can peek over the bow as the water moves under us.

"I think I just saw another fish!" he says. "Or maybe it was the one I set free! Maybe it's the only one in there, the poor thing. I bet it can't see a thing in all that sludge."

He starts to reach forward to put his fingers in the water.

"Don't!" I yell.

He jumps.

"Hen, it's really dirty. You'd probably get a disease or something."

"But I touched the fish! How's that different?"

"You had to," I say. "But you probably shouldn't do it again."

Henry fake-shivers and goes back to searching for life under the surface.

I wonder if Gus is down there, looking up at us. I wonder if he was reincarnated as a fish, and he can finally swim out of here. I wonder if he is our fish, and we just set him free.

chapter nine

After we lock up the boat, we head back to the house. Henry sets the remaining worm free in the garden while I put Gus's fishing pole and tackle box back in the garage. As I walk past Gus's car, I glance inside. Gus used one of those wooden, beaded seat covers. I always wondered if it was comfortable. I look closer through the window and see all the familiar pieces of Gus inside. The change from the MiniMart in the open ashtray holder that he emptied once a week when it got full. When I was younger, he'd let me count it out and sometimes buy a treat with it. I put my hand on the glass and leave a print on the dusty window. Dusty already. I check to see if Henry is coming before I open the door and get behind the wheel.

I lean against the worn, wooden beads and grasp the steering wheel. The car smells like pine freshener and hot vinyl. On the passenger seat is an old, neatly folded blue-and-green knitted blanket that my grandmother made. I reach over and touch the soft yarn. I wonder if Gus did the same thing whenever he got in the car. An over-powering sense of loneliness creeps around me at the thought. I squeeze the steering wheel, imagining Gus's hands touching the same gray rubber grip. If I had the keys, it would be so simple to drive away. To disappear for real.

There's a quiet knock on the passenger door window. Henry's sweaty face peers in at me.

I nod.

He picks up the blanket as he gets inside and places it on his lap.

His fingers gently thrum the top of the blanket as he waits for me to say something.

"I wish I tried to spend more time with him," I finally say.

Henry breathes in slowly. He seems uncomfortable, like maybe he agrees with me and doesn't know what to say.

"He must have been so lonely, you know? My mom was right. He didn't have any friends. I should have talked to him more. I should have tried harder. Every time I think of him all I can see is the sadness in his eyes. I can *feel* the loneliness of him. It's in his room. In his living room chair. In the boat. It's in *here*. I can feel it right *now*. Can't you?"

Henry glances around. "Sort of."

I rub my arms even though I'm not cold. "There's this sad nothingness that was here before he left, and now that he's gone, it's even stronger. Like a horrible sadness that keeps getting bigger."

Even as I say the words, I feel my own loneliness taking hold, like a cold shadow blanket wrapping itself around me, urging me to disappear once and for all.

"Bean. You think Gus was sad because you miss him and it's sad that he died. But it's not your fault if he was lonely."

The back of my throat aches from trying not to cry.

"Do you know that I can't even remember the last time I saw Gus laugh? I swear, Henry. I can't remember! I don't even know what he looked like when he was happy. Maybe he never was! Not since before my grandmother died!"

My throat gives up and I let myself cry. Henry reaches over and puts a hand on my thigh and squeezes. It's something Sally does when we're watching a particularly sad scene on *Days*. "I bet he laughed a few times. I bet, maybe, when he went down to the MiniMart and got his coffee in the morning, that lady at the counter, what's her name?"

"Susie?"

"Yeah, Susie. I bet she made him laugh. She makes everyone laugh. I bet he was her special challenge or something."

"Maybe."

"Come on, Bean." He squeezes my thigh again. "Don't feel guilty. You two always got along. He and your mom are another story, it's true. But that's not *your* fault. I don't think *anyone* could've gotten them to make peace."

"You know what his last words to me were?"

I feel sweat gathering between the bare skin on my leg and his hand. Besides my hand, I think this is the first time Henry has touched me skin to skin on purpose. I know it's just a comfort touch, but it still feels strange.

"No," he says.

"Be good."

Henry looks out the passenger side window at the row of recycling bins lining the wall.

I touch the pearl earrings I still haven't taken out. "I think what he really meant was, *Don't be like your mom.* I think he was afraid I'd make the same mistakes. Like I'd get pregnant and end up being a waitress all my life."

Henry unrolls the window and leans his face out to get some fresh air, only the air in the garage is musty and makes him cough.

I bite my lip and wait for him to breathe normally again.

"Maybe . . . maybe he just meant to be good. Like, have a good day and don't get into trouble. I mean, it's not like he knew those would be his last words, right?"

I close my eyes and think. I try to remember Gus's eyes when he said those words. Did he know somehow? Did he want those to be his last words to me? Was he trying to tell me something?

"Do you think it really was my mom's fault, Hen?"

"What do you mean?"

"Her getting pregnant." I concentrate on the dashboard. "Do you think she was raped or do you think she made the whole thing up? I mean, she knew the guy. *Bill.* My dad. But that's not what she let on to Gus."

Henry and I haven't talked about our dads since I told him about the conversation I overheard when I was twelve. Once my dream dad was shattered, it didn't seem fair to talk about Henry's dream dad. Besides, if my dad could turn out to be a total loser, so could Henry's. It was best to protect the dream by not talking about it.

Henry takes a careful breath and manages not to cough again. "I'm not sure, Bean." He picks at the cracked vinyl on the armrest. "Do you really want to know?"

I let the question sink in. "Sometimes I do. But sometimes I wish I didn't know anything at all."

"Yeah. Me too." He inspects his fingernails and picks a tiny piece of vinyl from one. He wipes it on his shorts underneath the folded blanket that's still resting on his lap. He sighs and pulls his shirt away from his body. "Hot in here," he says, shifting the blanket uncomfortably.

I take the blanket from him and place it on the backseat. As I reach, I have to move closer to him, I smell his sweat and a hint of cologne. My stomach twists in a funny way. I quickly lean away. When I do, I feel the sweat on my own back and wonder if I'll have a sweat spot through my T-shirt.

"We better go," I say.

Henry nods and opens the door. As we walk toward the house, I make sure to stand behind him just in case there's a spot. He turns to make sure I'm coming.

"Want to stick around for a while?" I ask, catching up to him.

"Sure," he says. "But this time, no wine."

"No," I say. "Definitely not."

chapter ten

There's laughter coming from the kitchen when we get back to the house. I roll my eyes at Henry and check my watch. It isn't even noon yet and they're already drinking. I'm sure of it.

"Sally, you look *amazing*!" my mom shrieks.

Henry gives me a quick, raised eyebrow.

Sally's out again?

We rush to the kitchen.

Sally is sitting on a stool at the kitchen sink. Her large bottom covers the whole seat so just the stool legs stick out from under her. My mom has most of Sally's newly bleached-blond hair in her hands, twisting it up on top of her head while Claire applies mascara to her eyelashes.

Henry's mouth drops open and stays there.

"Whoa," I say out loud by mistake.

All three of them freeze and look at us. I swear the

clock in the hallway goes into slow motion, waiting for a response. It's a standoff.

"What *happened*?" Henry asks, as if Sally had shaved her head.

I step closer to get a better look. Without her dark hair poofed up on top the way it usually is, Sally seems lighter. Like a giant white lily with pink streaks. Her cheeks have too much blush. She looks like a Barbie experiment gone wrong. Like she got microwaved and blew up and her face got all out of proportion.

She smiles weakly at us.

"It's makeover day," my mom says, ignoring our obvious looks of disapproval and, well, horror. "I'm next!"

Terrific.

I can only imagine what they'll do to her if this is what they've come up with for Sally.

"Doesn't she look *beautiful*?" Claire asks. I've never seen Claire smile in such a genuinely happy way. Maybe she should change careers and be a stylist. Or not.

Sally blushes at the new word most likely never used to describe her. She touches her hair and looks at Henry hopefully.

Henry finally closes his mouth and appears to swallow. "Wow," he says.

First off, Sally is in our kitchen for the second time in two days. She's out of the house for a second day in a row. And now this. I think it might be too much for Henry to take.

73

Sally touches her hair again and smiles at Henry. There are tears in her eyes.

"Blond," she says, like she can't believe it. "Do you like it, Hen?"

Henry manages to nod at the stranger in front of us.

"Beany?" Sally looks at me with the same, hopeful eyes. I touch her hair gingerly and force myself to nod like Henry. She smiles back and her whole body seems to glow.

I quickly glance over at my mom, whose own face is glowing just as brightly. Why is everyone so *happy*?

"Okay. Sal gal, get on up off that stool and give me a turn," my mom says.

Sal gal? What the hell is happening here?

"Mom," I say, "you're already blond."

"I know," she says. "And now I'm going red."

She holds up a box of Clairol and shakes it, smiling. She *never* would have done this if Gus was here.

And that's when I finally understand. That's why she's so happy. It's hard to think of Sally and my mom having anything in common, but they do. Suddenly, they're both free.

Claire helps my mom arrange a towel over her shoulders to protect her shirt from the dye. "*I'm* going black," she says.

What a surprise.

I watch as she takes control, gently guiding my mom's head back under the faucet. Sally stands to the side, beaming at them. Henry leans against the counter, apparently still recovering from the shock of seeing Sally, here, in our kitchen. Blond.

"Well, have fun," I say sarcastically. I can't help it. This just doesn't seem right. Everything—everyone—is changing. Literally. And while they may *look* happy, I'm not sure if it's for the better.

I turn around and walk out, hoping Henry will follow.

But he doesn't.

I walk through the living room and keep my eyes from looking at Gus's empty chair.

In the hallway upstairs, Gus's door is closed again so I open it. Then I go inside and lie down on his white cotton bedspread. It's one of those old-fashioned chenille spreads with the tiny ball things on it. When I was little I used to sneak in the room while Gus was out and lie on the bed and pick at the balls with my fingers.

I look up at the ceiling light and imagine Gus doing the same thing, night after night. I imagine him lying awake, staring at the light, thinking about . . . things. Maybe wondering about my mom and why she acts the way she does. Maybe about me, and why I act the way I do. Maybe he wondered why I seemed to have only one friend. Maybe he thought about my grandmother, and how much he wished she was still here. Thinking about her, I wonder if *she* stared up at this light when she couldn't sleep, too, wondering about the future and, when she knew she was dying, if my mom would be okay. I think about how all of our eyes have settled on this same spot. This one, old light with the frosted white glass. I spread my arms out to either side of me, my fingers outstretched, like I'm making an angel in the snow. As I move my arms, I feel the empty spaces where my grandparents have both lain. I stretch my fingers out and concentrate as hard as I can on the light that holds us all together in memory, willing myself to feel them both if only for a second. Then, maybe I could feel real myself.

"What are you doing?"

I jump into a sitting position.

Henry looks at me from the open doorway as if I've lost my mind.

"Nothing," I say.

He steps into the room and looks around.

"I've never been in here."

"It's nice, isn't it?"

"Yeah."

"Wanna sit?"

"Okay."

I move over. He sits next to me on the bed. I lean back and put my head on one pillow, and he does the same. We stare up at the light.

"This is weird," he says.

"Everything's weird," I say.

"Yeah. My mom."

"I know."

"She looks ridiculous," he says quietly.

"I know."

"Do you think they're really going to be, like, friends with her now?"

"I guess. I'm not sure." I feel myself getting annoyed with my mom and Claire again. I'm sure they think they're Sally's saviors now, having gotten her out of the house with such ease. But she came out first for *me*, not them.

Oh.

Crap.

"This is all my fault."

"What do you mean?"

"I asked Sally to come to the funeral. If she hadn't come, she'd still be at home and everything would be normal."

"Normal?"

"You know what I mean."

He keeps staring at the light. "I guess I should be glad she's out. I just hope . . . she doesn't get hurt."

Exactly.

I move my head so I'm facing him.

"You know why I think she never left the house till now?" he asks.

I shake my head.

"She's been waiting."

"Waiting for what?"

He swallows loudly, like he has a pre-cry lump in his throat. "My dad."

"Oh."

"So I was thinking, you know, with her being here now,

and not home? I'm thinking maybe she's finally given up. Maybe she's decided it's safe to leave the house. Maybe she's finally realized he's never coming back."

He rubs his eyes as if he's trying not to cry. I want to reach out to him, but I'm not sure where to touch.

"Hen. That's not really a bad thing, is it? Her finally realizing it's true?"

He nods but stays quiet for a while, as if he's the one finally realizing. "I thought it would be," he says, "a good thing. When I heard her name when we came in, I felt glad that she was here. But then when I saw her . . . Bean, I mean, she looks *horrible*. Like way worse than any soap star she idolizes. Like she's a joke! Your mom wouldn't do that, would she? Make a big joke out of my mom?"

"Of course not! God, Henry. My mom is whacked but she isn't mean."

"Sorry. It's just that—how could they really think she looks good?"

"Maybe they just think different is good. No matter what."

"I guess. Maybe the two of us should dye our hair, too."

"Ha ha. Maybe we should shave our heads."

He touches his buzz cut and laughs.

"I mean *all the way*. As in *bald*."

"Not gonna happen."

"Yeah, me neither."

We lay there quietly for a while. A gentle breeze drifts through the window and over us like an invisible moving blanket. Every so often our peaceful moment is interrupted by an exaggerated high-pitched screech through the floorboards, indicating, most likely, that my mom is now a redhead.

Henry sighs heavily beside me. He's so close I can feel his body warmth and hear the occasional gurgles inside his stomach. He holds his hand over it to try to muffle the sound. I want to tell him I don't mind it. I even like his raspy asthma breath.

I close my eyes and listen to that steady breathing.

When I wake up, Henry is gone and I have a soft blanket over me. I'm sweating.

I listen for signs of annoying women in the kitchen but I don't hear anything, just the *tock tock tock* of the clock downstairs, echoing through the house. I roll over and smell the bleachy white bedspread, then hear the click of a light switch.

"What are you doing in here?"

My mom stands in the doorway, looking like she's seen a ghost. I squint in the sudden brightness of the room.

I sit up quickly.

"Jesus, Beany. I thought you were at Henry's. I was just coming to shut this damn door."

"Why?"

"Why what?" Her hair is conveniently tucked under a hot-pink bandanna, but I can see a wisp of bright red sticking out.

"Why do you shut his door?"

She scratches her head through her bandanna and winces. "I don't like it open," she says.

"Well, I do," I say.

"Get out of this room." She puts her hands on her hips but stays in the doorway.

"No."

"Beany, I'm not kidding. I know you're grieving, but I don't want you in here. It isn't right."

"What's not right about it?"

"Look at you! You're on his bed, for God's sake!"

"So what! It makes me feel close to him. To them."

"To *them*? Are you kidding me?"

"No! What's wrong with that?"

"Everything! Just get out of there. Now."

"No, Mom." It feels strange to call her Mom. I think this is about the longest conversation we've had in days. Maybe weeks. Maybe even months. I can tell by the way she looks at me that she thinks I'm a freak. But I guess she's always felt that way.

"Beany," she says, still not stepping inside the door. "Don't make me come in there."

Or what? I don't say. I imagine my mom trying to drag me out of the room. It's a pathetic sight.

"Don't make me leave!" I say.

"Fine! You want to act all crazy? Go ahead! I don't need this!"

She turns and disappears from the doorway. I listen for

her footsteps, waiting for them to move down the hall, but they don't. She's waiting.

I look around the room and suddenly feel like I don't belong, and I hate my mom for making me feel that way. I rush to the hallway and almost slam into her. She's standing with her arms crossed at her chest. I don't meet her eyes. I just walk to my room. But before I go in, I turn to face her. "At least leave his door open," I say.

She turns away from me without answering.

I slam my own door shut.

chapter eleven

It feels like early evening when I finally creep out of my room. I go downstairs to find something to eat and, big surprise, there's Claire heating up leftovers for a late-night meal.

"So, are you moving in or something?" I ask. I'm not usually this rude, but Claire's presence is really starting to get to me, like everything else.

"Your mom needs me to be here. Can't you see that?"

No. I can't.

A strong whiff of leftover lasagna reaches my nose. I make a face that I'm sure is unattractive. "Where is she, anyway?" I ask.

"Up on the roof. She told me to send you up when you came out of your room."

"She's on the roof?"

"Yeah. Don't tell me you don't know she goes there."

I shrug. "Of course I know," I lie. "I just . . . didn't think she'd be there now."

Claire studies me for a minute, like she knows I'm lying. "Well, she is. And I know she'd probably like to talk about things with you."

She turns away from me to stir something in a pot. She doesn't seem like she really knows what she's doing. Her new hair is jet-black. Spiky and short like a guy's. I don't know what look she was going for, but it wasn't successful. The back of her neck is blackish purple where the dye dribbled down and stained her skin. God, she looks bad.

"Okay, well, I guess I'll go up there then," I say.

I leave her in the kitchen and go upstairs. I don't know how my mom got on the roof, but I'm determined to figure it out without having to ask Claire.

From the top of the stairs, the door to the bathroom is straight ahead. The light is on and the window and screen are open.

I stop at Gus's closed door and touch the handle, but something stops me from opening it. Instead, I go to the bathroom and peek my head out the open window and see her silhouette. She's sitting way over to the left, leaning against the slanted roof. Her body is dark, like a shadow, in the deep shade of the tree. With her ponytail profile, she looks like a young girl.

"Come on out here," she says without turning her head to see that it's me. She doesn't sound mad anymore.

"How did you know I was here?" I ask.

"I could feel you."

I pause at that one, and my heart warms up just a little. I lean farther out the window and eye the slanting roof I'd have to crawl across to get to where she is.

"I don't think I can come out there."

"Oh, come on, live a little. It's not as steep as it looks." She pats the space next to her for me. I don't think she has ever done that before and I'm immediately suspicious. However, there is no way I'm going to let my mom be braver than I am, so I hoist myself up and squeeze through the window. The shingles are still warm from the day's sun and rough under my hands as I crawl on all fours to her. I sit close enough to smell her watermelon hair spray that doesn't quite conceal the chemical smell of hair dye.

"Claire told me you come out here all the time," I say. "I didn't know that."

"Claire said that? No. I used to. But I haven't been out here in—" She lifts her head to the branches above. "Wow. Not since I was pregnant with you."

"But that was fifteen years ago."

"I know. I used to come out here a lot when I was your age. Your grandmother showed me how when I was about ten. Gus had yelled at me for something and I told her I was going to run away. I'd packed up my pink Barbie suitcase and headed down the street. Mom drove up behind me and talked me into coming back home. Then she walked me up to the window and pointed to this very spot and said next time, instead of running away, to come on out here and tell my angry thoughts to the leaves. She said the leaves were the tree's ears. Isn't that funny?"

I shake my head.

"She was starting to get really sick then. She went downhill so fast. The sicker she got, the more time I spent out here, just waiting. We knew she was going to die. And I was pretty sure that without her, *I* would die. At least inside. I couldn't imagine what life would be like without her."

I feel the loneliness blanket spread over me again, smothering me. Dead while living. It makes me think of Gus.

"Why did you stop coming out here?" I ask to break the quiet.

She half laughs, but it sounds like she's more sad than amused. "I couldn't fit through the window. Then, after I had you, I felt like I should be a grown-up. The leaves didn't seem like ears anymore. I knew they weren't listening. And even if they were, they sure as hell couldn't help me."

The blanket goes up over my head. I can't breathe. I imagine my mom so trapped she couldn't even escape to her fake runaway place. And it was all my fault.

"I really ruined your life, didn't I?" I say. And I feel it so strongly. How I changed everything for the worse. I understand why she never felt like I imagined a mother should. How could she?

She turns and looks me in the eye for the first time in a long, long time. "I won't lie to you. At the time? Yes. I thought my life was over because of you. And life as I knew it *was* over. But come on, Bean. It's not like you had any control over your existence. That was my own doing."

"It still sucks to know your existence ruined people's lives."

"You didn't ruin people's lives. You just changed them. Eventually for the better. I mean, honestly, I was not going down a very pretty road when you came along. In fact, I think you probably saved me." She lifts her arm and carefully puts it over my shoulder. I try hard to concentrate on the foreign feeling of her hand pressing into me, connecting us.

"I'm sorry for earlier," she says. "I wasn't expecting to find you in Gus's room. I guess I overreacted."

"It's okay," I say. Her hand feels heavy on me. I try to feel her energy passing through to me, like I do when Sally touches me, but I don't. It's the way we've always been with each other. Too distant to feel, even when we're touching.

We sit quietly for a while, not telling the leaves anything at all.

"Why did you come back up here tonight?" I finally ask. "Do you feel like running away again?"

I picture my mom and Claire running off in my mom's car like in *Thelma and Louise*, one of my mom's favorite old movies.

"Not at all! I don't know why I came back here, actually. I guess with Gus gone, I feel like taking back all the things he stole."

"What did he steal, Mom?"

She's quiet for a minute. "My childhood. Who I am. Who I want to be."

For what feels like the thousandth time, I try to imagine how my Gus and her Gus could be the same person. "How did he do that?"

"By not understanding. Not listening. By making me hide—" She stops.

"Hide what?"

She sighs. "Oh, I don't know. Let's talk about something else, huh?"

I want to ask her about my grandmother. I want to be brave and ask her about me. And my father. But instead I sit quietly next to her. For the first time, she feels like she *could* be that mom I always imagined. Someone you can talk to. Someone who can put her arm around you. Almost.

"Food's ready!" Claire's voice pierces through our perfect moment. The leaves shudder.

"Be there in a minute!" my mom calls cheerfully.

She takes her arm back and pats my thigh. "You come out here when you need to think," she says. "I'm officially leaving this place to you now."

"But it's yours."

"I don't need it anymore. Sometimes you have to take

things back before you can let them go. I just came up to say good-bye. I'm happy now, Bean. Not because Gus died. I know you find that hard to believe. But I'm free now. That's honestly how I feel. I don't need to hide up here anymore."

"But I do?"

"You're a teenager." She shoves me a little with her shoulder. "Next time you get mad at me, do me a favor and come out here instead of going into Gus's room."

I ignore that.

"C'mon, let's go get rid of those gawd-awful leftovers."

She stands and walks bravely across the slanted roof while I crawl behind her.

Back inside, I follow her down the hallway. When we pass Gus's door, I pause and open it.

"We need to talk about that," my mom says.

But she doesn't close the door.

chapter twelve

As we make our way downstairs, the clock chimes its half-song to let us know it's six-thirty. I follow my mom into the kitchen.

"What's cooking, sweetie?" my mom asks.

My mom and Claire are like the teen best friends I'll never have. The kind that paint each other's nails, do each other's hair, have sleepovers, stay up late, and sneak drinks from their parents' liquor cabinet. Okay, well, Henry and I have done that last one. But sometimes I wish Henry was a girl so we could do all that other stuff.

"Leftovers and edamame," Claire says. Ew. "But later I'll make popcorn for the movie."

"Movie?" My mom grins excitedly.

"Yup. And it's a good one so let's eat fast."

"You want to join us later, Beany?" my mom asks. "We could have a pajama party."

I knew it. They are such teenagers.

"Can I invite Henry?"

"Of course. In fact, invite Sally too. Forget the pajamas. We'll just have a regular old movie party."

After dinner I help my mom clean up while Claire makes her stupid popcorn the old-fashioned way on the stovetop. Her shoulders shake extra hard as she jiggles the pan over the burner. The kernels start to pop one at a time, then faster.

"We have the microwave kind," I say to her back.

"It's not the same," she says. "You're about to enjoy the best popcorn you've ever had."

"Wait for Henry and Sally," my mom says, coming up behind her and peeking excitedly at the lidded pot like it holds gold instead of popcorn. "Go call them quick, Beany."

I leave Claire and my mom in the kitchen and call Henry.

"You want me and my mom to come over *now*?" he asks.

"Yes?"

"Hang on."

I listen hard while he goes to ask Sally about the spontaneous party. I can tell they're arguing, the way their voices go back and forth so quickly, but I can't tell who wants to come and who doesn't.

"Okay," Henry says when he comes back to the phone. "We'll be there soon."

I wait for him to click off before I hang up, too.

"They're coming!" I call as I head back to the kitchen.

My mom is standing close behind Claire at the table while Claire pours melted butter over an enormous wooden bowl of popcorn. She jumps back quickly at the sound of my voice.

"What?" I ask.

"N-nothing!" my mom says. Her cheeks are bright pink.

"I didn't want you to see my secret ingredient," Claire says kind of quickly.

"What are you going to do, poison me?"

My mom laughs. "Honestly, Bean."

"Turn around while I put it in," Claire says.

"Okay, but I'm going to make you eat some of it before I do." I turn around while Claire and my mom fumble around with something on the counter.

"All right, you can come taste now," my mom says.

Before I get to the bowl, both my mom and Claire scoop out handfuls and start eating.

"Mmmmm," my mom says, smiling at Claire. "Definitely the best I've ever had. You've gotta try it, Bean."

"Okay, okay." I take one piece and carefully put it in my mouth. It's salty and sweet and buttery and—ugh—delicious, even though I don't want it to be and definitely don't want to admit it.

"What did you do to it?" I ask. Isn't arsenic supposed to have a sweet taste?

"Butter, salt, and sugar. Isn't it perfect?"

"Not bad," I say.

"You love it. Admit it," my mom says, grinning at me.

She bumps hips with Claire before they saunter off into the other room to set up the movie.

I stay in the kitchen sneaking bites of the popcorn. When the doorbell rings I pick up the bowl and carry it to the front door.

"Welcome!" I say, happy to have someone normal back in the house.

Henry looks at me suspiciously. Sally stands behind him with her yellow hair piled on top of her head. I'm glad to see her, even though she does look insane with that hair. She's wearing a muumuu-type dress that floats around her, making her look like one of those tacky dolls they sell on QVC, with the big skirts you put over spare toilet-paper rolls.

"Hi, hon," Sally says. She's carrying a family-size bag of Doritos. The bag reminds me of Sally's house. I haven't been there since the day after Gus died.

"What're we watching?" Henry asks as they come inside.

"Um. I'm not sure."

Henry raises his eyebrows doubtfully.

"Sorry. Guess I should've asked."

"Yeah."

"There she is!" Claire yells when the three of us reach the living room, apparently all invisible except for Sally.

"You look wonderful, Sally!" my mom says. She twists a very red lock of her own, new hair. "I'm so glad you came."

Sally nods and sits in the middle of the couch, holding the bag of Doritos in her lap.

"I'll get a bowl for those," I say, putting the popcorn down on the coffee table and taking the bag from Sally.

"You *have* to try Claire's popcorn," my mom says as I leave the room.

Henry follows me into the kitchen. Already we can hear our moms laughing in the living room. Then the sticky slap of bare feet in flip-flops comes down the hallway.

"Drinks for everyone!" Claire says in a sing-song voice as she makes her way to the fridge and opens the freezer. She pulls out a new bottle of vodka and sets it on the counter. Then she gets three tall glasses from the cupboard.

I roll my eyes at Henry while Claire rummages for cranberry juice and a lime in the fridge.

We wait for Claire to finish and then find some opaque plastic glasses, which we fill with Kool-Aid and some of the vodka. I stand lookout at the door while Henry mixes the drinks. When he finishes, he hands me mine and we go back to the pathetic party in the living room.

Claire is fussing with the DVD player while my mom fidgets with Sally's hair.

"Oops! I forgot the Doritos!" I say. I go back to the kitchen to find a bowl. When I return, my mom is standing behind Henry, pushing her fingers through his stubby hair. There's a tube of hair gel on the table. Henry is cringing.

"What are you doing?" I ask.

"I was just seeing what he'd look like with his hair a bit spikier," my mom says.

First of all, Henry's hair is basically a crew cut, so there isn't much to spike. Second of all, watching your mom play with your best friend's hair is creepy.

"Well, don't please," I say. "He likes it the way it is."

"Fine." She takes her hands away, and Henry quickly darts his head out from under them.

"Come on, let's start the movie," Claire says, pulling my mom's arm and leading her away from Henry.

"What are we watching, anyway?" I ask.

"*An Affair to Remember*," my mom says wistfully.

"Oooh," Sally says from the couch. "I love that movie. Cary Grant and Deborah Kerr." She sighs.

"But you've seen that a million times!" I whine.

"And I could watch it a million more," my mom says.

I plop myself down next to Sally and lean forward for a big handful of popcorn. Then I take a long, defiant drink from my plastic cup.

Henry follows my lead.

Once everyone's settled, Claire turns off the lights and starts the movie.

Henry, Sally, and I sit on the couch in our usual positions. Only we're in the wrong place. We're in Bizarro World.

Claire and my mom sit on the floor in front of the coffee table, using it to lean their backs on. My mom settles her head on Claire's shoulder like she's her date.

I take another drink. And another.

Every time I lean forward for more popcorn I feel light-headed. I wonder if the joke is lost on everyone but me that we are all sitting here watching a romantic movie about true love when not one of us has ever experienced it and probably never will.

I lean my head back and close my eyes. Sally quietly chews popcorn while the bowl of Doritos remains untouched. Henry fidgets with his shirt and continues to look tortured. Claire and my mom make "aw" and "oh" and "I love this part" noises from the floor.

In the crowded room, I feel very lonely.

Gus's empty chair looks at me. Why didn't we do this when you were here? I think. What were we so afraid of?

When the movie is finally over, Claire gets up to fill my mom's and Sally's drinks. My head is spinning and I just want to go to bed. But Sally doesn't look like she plans on leaving anytime soon, so that means Henry won't be either.

"Come on," I say to him.

He follows me out to the front porch, and we sit on the steps. It's hot and humid, and the cicadas are buzzing away. A moth circles the porch light, hitting it over and over again with a quiet thwack.

"That movie was depressing," Henry says, watching the moth.

It's true. I know the ending is supposed to be happy, but all I can remember when the movie ends is the pain and frustration I feel when Terry doesn't show up to meet her true love on top of the Empire State Building. I mean, even though in the end it's all okay. I can't get over that moment. My mom insists that it is the most romantic movie ever made and rents it at least once a year, crying the whole way through. Except that this time I didn't notice a single tear until the end, when there's no reason to be sad.

"Do you think we'll always stay friends?" Henry asks. "I mean, after we graduate and stuff?"

"Of course," I say. "We're all we have."

"Seriously though. Even when we're in college? What if we go to different schools?"

"What makes you think college is going to bring us new friends? If we're this socially challenged now, college will be even worse, I'm sure."

Henry flaps his shirt. "What are you talking about?"

"Think about it. We've been all the way through elementary school and part of high school, right? We've known these people all our lives and haven't managed to break into the fold. In college, you only get four years. If it's taken us all our lives to get this far, do you really think we're going to score a posse in college?"

"You're crazy."

"I'm right."

"Well, if we go to different schools we better stay friends then," he says.

"Of course."

"And we'll meet somewhere when we graduate. Like on July first. Just like in the movie."

"Definitely," I say. "How about at the top of the Empire State Building?"

"Right. Naturally."

"I'm glad that's settled," I say. And I really hope that it is. Because even though my mom says she's happy now, I don't want to ever feel trapped like her. Or Gus.

Henry leans back on his elbows, which rest on the top step. A second moth joins the first, and they do a sort of dance, taking turns thwacking into the light.

"They're like us," Henry says.

"Who?"

"The moths."

"Why?"

"Hopeless."

I lean back next to Henry. Inside, our moms and Claire are playing a drinking game. A quarter smacks against a counter and my mom yells, "Drink!" God, they are so juvenile.

The moths bump bump against the light.

Maybe he's right.

chapter thirteen

We sit for a long time, not talking. Just listening to the inside noises. I don't want to go back in there. I pick at a scab on my knee and watch a speck of blood ooze up. Henry pushes the cuticles back on each finger.

"Let's go for a walk," I say. I have no idea where we can walk this late at night. There's noplace safe around here anymore.

"We can't," Henry says. "There's nowhere to go."

"Then let's sneak up to my room. Anything. I can't stand sitting here watching the bugs fly toward the light another second."

We creep back into the house, careful not to let the screen door slam.

Our moms and Claire are still partying it up in the kitchen. We could've slammed the door and they wouldn't have noticed.

I climb the stairs first. In the upstairs hallway, Gus's door is closed again. Instead of going to my room, I stand in the doorway, staring at the grain in the wooden door.

Henry comes up behind me. "What are you doing?"

I open the door. "She keeps shutting it."

"Who?"

"My mom. Or Claire, I guess."

"I can see why."

"Why?"

"It's spooky," he says. He steps back, as if saying the words makes it even more so.

"Well, I'm keeping it open. My mom might want to shut him out but I don't."

"Bean, just leave it." He puts his hand on the doorknob.

I ignore him and go inside before he can close the door. The room feels even more still and stopped in time than it did before. A light breeze sends the white curtains dancing gently. But the room is starting to smell stale, even with the open windows.

The sides of my mouth quiver. Gus is fading.

I sit on the edge of the bed. I don't try to hide my face from Henry when I feel my tears come.

"Hey," he says from the doorway. "Are you okay? Why don't you come out of there?"

I shake my head. It's not spooky in here. It's just empty. There's no ghost.

No bits of Gus.

He got out of here at last.

I move back on the bed and rest my head on the head-board. I still feel a little dizzy from the vodka.

Henry slowly forces himself into the room and sits down next to me. His sweat smells sweet.

I lean my head into his neck and feel his friendship folding into me.

The corner streetlamp shines through the open window and turns the objects in the room to shadows.

Henry sighs heavily next to me. I imitate him. He does it again so I do too. We laugh a little. Then he slowly reaches for my hand. In the dark, I can just make out the shadow of our hands together. I feel a slow warmth spread up my arm. It feels foreign and familiar at the same time.

I squeeze his hand lightly and close my eyes.

"Thanks for being my best friend," I say.

He squeezes back. "No problem."

I listen to the rhythm of his breath and feel his hand in mine. I don't dare open my eyes, or speak, or move. I want to just *be*. Here. With Henry.

"What the hell are you doing in here?"

I jump a mile at my mom's voice. A sweaty hand slips out of mine. My head has been resting on Henry's shoulder.

Henry stands up in a flash. My mom flicks on the light and blinds us. Squinting, Henry tries to get his footing.

"We fell asleep, that's all," I say, standing up.

"In *here*?" my mom asks.

She doesn't look like a teenager anymore. She looks like an angry, old adult. She looks suspicious. She looks like . . . like Gus used to when she came home late.

Claire appears behind her in the hall. She gives me a disapproving look.

"We weren't doing anything!" I yell. "We came in here to get away from *you*!" I hope Claire realizes I mean that in the plural.

"Oh, really?" My mom wobbles a little. I can smell the alcohol on her breath.

"Yes! This is the only peaceful room in this entire house if you want to know the truth!"

Henry fumbles with his shirt, which has come untucked. The gesture does not help our case, clearly, as my mom glares at him.

"I am so disappointed in you, Beany. And in *here* of all places. That's it. I'm moving all this crap out of here tomorrow."

"What? No! You can't do that!"

"This is . . . this is sick, you in here. On this bed!"

"Sick? What do you think we were doing, Mom? We fell *asleep*!"

"I'm supposed to believe that?"

"Yes! I'm not *you*!"

She steps back, her mouth open.

It's as if my words just punched her in the face.

She raises her hand as if to slap me back with a real hand, but Claire grabs her shoulders and holds her. My mom has never hit me before, but I'm sure if Claire hadn't grabbed hold I'd be toast. It's like the anger she's held inside her entire life has come bubbling up to the surface, and it is directed at me. It's all because of me, whatever she says.

"Everything all right?" Sally's voice calls from downstairs.

No one answers.

My mom steps back into the hall and lets Claire embrace her.

"Overreact much?" I say.

"I can't believe you would do this." She looks from me to Henry. "I thought you two were just friends. If I'd known, I would have—"

"We *are* just friends!" I scream. "Why won't you believe me? God, Mom. This is pretty ironic coming from you. For someone who hated how Gus treated you, you sure are good at treating me the same way!"

My mom glares at me. I wait for her to yell back, but instead I see the realization of what I just said take hold. She sags into Claire's arms and starts to cry.

"Oh, God," she sobs. "You're right."

I step away from her and bump into Henry, who I didn't realize was standing right behind me. He puts his hand on my shoulder.

"She isn't right, Lexie. Jesus," Claire says. "Your mother is *nothing* like that man!" She yells at me. She actually looks like she might cry, too.

But my mom moves away from her. "I'm sorry, Beany. I—I saw the two of you and panicked. I just don't want you to make the same mistake I did."

Henry's hand on my shoulder tightens as her words sink in. I will myself not to let her or Claire see me cry.

"No, we have enough mistakes in this house, don't we?" I say.

My mom looks horrified. "Oh, Bean, that's not what I meant!"

"But it's true! You said I saved you, but I'm still just a mistake in the end. That's what I'll always be to you. Your big mistake!"

"No, Bean. Not you."

"Never mind." I have to get away from her.

"You better take Sally home, Hen," I say quietly. He nods but doesn't take his hand off me so I reach up and move it for him. Before I let go, I look him in the eye and nod to let him know I'm okay. He nods back. I walk past my mom and Claire and go to my room, making a point to shut my door as quietly as I can, as if I don't exist.

chapter fourteen

I wake up to my mom's and Claire's voices. They're arguing. I can't understand why Claire's staying over again. It's starting to feel weird. Everything feels weird.

I look down at my hand and remember Henry's in it. The warmth, and how our hands were stuck together when we woke up. Like they were melting together. I call him without checking what time it is.

"Hello?" His voice is groggy.

"It's me."

"What time is it?"

"Early. What are you doing?"

"Trying to sleep?"

"Oh. Right. Sorry."

"Are you okay? Did your mom calm down?"

"She and Claire are arguing now."

"Oh. Um. You didn't answer me."

"What?"

"I asked if you were okay."

I look at my hand again.

"Yes. I'm okay," I say. "Can you come over?"

"Now? It's like eight o'clock. Go back to sleep, Bean. I'm not coming over. If you're okay, that is. You sound okay."

I sigh.

"I am. I think my mom must be going back to work today. Maybe that's why she's up."

"No, she's taking my mom shopping."

"What?"

"Yeah. That's what Sally told me on the way home last night. Your mom decided to take the whole week off, and they're all going to the mall to celebrate."

"Well, Claire and my mom are still fighting, so I don't know if that's the plan."

"What are they fighting about?"

"I don't know." I bite the inside of my lip. "Do you think it's weird that Claire never goes home?"

"I guess so. Can I go back to sleep now?"

"Fine. I'll call you later." I hang up, feeling irritated with him. I don't know what I expected. Just . . . more.

I get out of bed and look out my window. I can see the river from here through the few trees that line the embankment. If Gus was alive, this would be the time of day he'd be out there. When the streets are still quiet.

I make my way to the shower and even though I'm hot, I turn the water almost as hot as it can go. I close my eyes and listen to the steady stream of water spray out of the faucet. There's an extra bottle of shampoo on the tray inside. And a new loofah sponge. And a third razor.

Claire appears to be here to stay.

Perfect.

When I finish I open the shower curtain. Water from the steam drips down the mirror, leaving a single streak. I feel sweaty before I even step out.

Back in my room, as I finish getting dressed, I hear the front door slam, then nothing. I wait, but the house is silent. I go downstairs to see if there's any leftover coffee. When I step into the kitchen, Claire is sitting quietly at the table. The coffeepot is empty. She looks up at me from the newspaper she's reading and raises her eyebrows.

"Where's my mom?" I ask.

"She went to get more coffee."

Her face is a little blotchy, as if she's been crying.

"I'm going to Henry's," I tell her.

She flattens her paper. "Do you think your mom would like that?"

I pause and turn back. "Do you think I care?" I snap.

She takes a sip of her coffee, just to rub it in, I'm sure.

"You should cut your mom some slack," she says.

"Why?"

"Because you don't know anything."

"Yeah, well, she's pretty clueless, too."

Claire shakes her head and rolls her eyes. "Someday you'll regret being so mean to her."

"Me? Mean to *her*? Are you *serious*?"

"You make assumptions, Bean. Be careful with that."

"Oh, and the two of you didn't make assumptions about me last night?"

"You were sleeping on your dead grandfather's bed with a boy. In the dark."

"He's my best friend! Whatever. I don't need to explain myself to you."

It feels strange to talk back to someone besides my mom. At the moment though, it feels good.

"Besides," I add, since I'm on a roll, "weren't you just fighting with her, too? Why is it okay for you to fight with her and not me?"

"We weren't fighting, we were arguing."

"Big difference," I say sarcastically.

"There is," she says. But judging from the cry splotches on her face, it's just as painful.

"Whatever," I say again. I leave her in the kitchen and head outside, but coming up the walk is Sally, all dressed up.

"Hi, Miss Bean," she says as she waddles up the walk to me. Her new blond hair is done up in a twist and she has so much makeup on she looks like a circus act. All she needs is a beard. God. What the hell is happening?

"Are the ladies up yet?" she asks. "We have a big day planned."

The *ladies*? I picture Claire with her spiky black hair. Hardly.

"Claire's in the kitchen," I say quietly. I'm still standing on the porch. Sally labors her way up the steps. I expect her to give me a hug or ask me how I'm doing, but she just smiles at me in her innocent way, like everything is perfectly normal and pleasant and she didn't overhear a word of what happened last night.

"We've got a shopping day planned. Did you know?" She is beaming.

Run, I want to tell her. *They don't deserve you.* I can see myself reaching for her hand and dragging her back home with me to Henry, but as I look at her hopeful face, I realize I probably wouldn't be able to move her one inch away from here.

As Sally continues to beam at me, my mom pulls into the driveway with a box of doughnuts from the MiniMart. She doesn't acknowledge me.

"Hi, honey!" Sally calls to her like she used to call to me when I visited. I feel a twinge. I want the old Sally back. The old Sally who belonged to me and Henry. Who sat on her big comfy sofa and patted the space next to her just for me.

When my mom steps onto the porch, she reaches over and gives Sally a kiss on the cheek. She has never kissed me on the cheek. Or anywhere else as far as I can remember.

"Join us for breakfast, Beany?" she asks nonchalantly. She doesn't meet my gaze, but I can tell this is her way of making a peace offering.

"No thanks," I say. I don't tell her where I'm headed and she doesn't ask.

"All right. We'll leave some for you in case you change your mind." She turns away and leads Sally inside.

The air is already steamy hot when I climb down the steps and head for Henry's house. I walk quickly, even though it's daytime and relatively safe. Gus says the city grew up around this neighborhood, then into it. But to me it feels like our quiet street is a small bubble trapped inside a bigger bubble. It seems like we are all trapped, one way or another.

chapter fifteen

"You're up," I tell Henry when I find him watching TV from his spot on the couch. He's wearing a white T-shirt and plaid pajama bottoms.

"Thanks for pointing that out." He doesn't look up at me.

"Sorry," I say. "Why are you watching *Good Morning America*? Sally isn't here."

"Something isn't right," he says, still staring at the TV.

"Yeah. You're watching *Good Morning America*," I tell him.

He's eating dry Cheerios from a plastic bowl. Henry wants to lose weight so desperately. He wants Sally to, too. But so far he hasn't had much luck in that department. I think, every time Henry looks at Sally, he fears what could happen to him.

"Want to go for a boat ride?" I ask. "No fishing, though. Just meandering."

Henry responds by pinching two Cheerios between his

fingers and slowly putting them in his mouth. He still hasn't looked at me.

"What is *wrong* with everyone today?"

He chews.

"Never mind." I leave him on the couch and start walking back toward my house. Maybe earlier was a dream, and when I go back, my mom will be sitting at the kitchen table—alone—with a cup of coffee and a frozen Snickers bar hidden under the morning paper.

No Sally.

No Claire.

I walk slowly, just in case. The neighborhood is quiet as usual, though someone at the end of the road is sweeping the sidewalk in front of his house and kicking up a small dust cloud that floats across the street like a ghost. That would please Gus, to see someone still caring about keeping things tidy. The swishing echoes up the street.

I'm halfway home when I hear shuffling feet and a familiar wheezing behind me.

I don't turn around, but it is the best sound I've heard in a long time.

"You need to get over the fish thing," Henry says, already flapping his shirt away from his body.

I grin at him.

"I'm just saying."

"You need to get over the not acknowledging me when I come over thing."

"Sorry. I was just . . . confused."

We stop walking and face each other. I squeeze my hand into a fist, remembering what his fingers felt like laced with mine. The heat of the pavement reaches up through my flip-flops.

"Everything's fine," I say.

He nods. "Okay."

We start walking again, this time side by side.

When we get back to my house, we're both sweating. My mom's car is gone.

"It's too hot to go out on the boat."

"Yeah."

"What do you want to do?"

"I don't know, what do you want to do?"

"I don't know, let's just go in."

"Hey," I say before we make our way up the steps.

Henry lowers his face and squints at me. His cheeks are getting pink. "What?"

"Thanks for coming after me."

He smiles. "Thanks for asking."

There's a note taped to the front door.

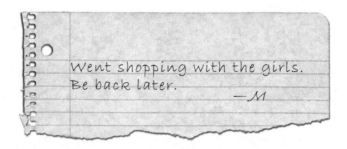

Went shopping with the girls.
Be back later.
          —M

M. Like it's too much work to write out *Mom*.

One time Gus told me that when I was learning to talk my mom tried to teach me to call her Lexie, not Mom. Maybe she thought if I called her Lexie, people would think she was my big sister and not my mom. She'd pat her chest and say, "Lexie?" But I'd point and say, "Ma-ma." I swear Gus thought this was so funny. But now, looking back, I just think it's really sad. Because even then, my mom didn't really want to be my mom. She just didn't know how.

I hold the note in my hands. "I don't get it. She knew I knew they were going shopping. Why the note?"

Henry shrugs. "Maybe she's trying to show you she isn't mad at you anymore. That she's talking to you again."

I think about her doughnut offer this morning. "She didn't have a reason to be mad at me in the first place. If anyone should be mad, it's me."

He shrugs. "It's just a note."

The sun is starting to bake the outdoors so we decide to sit in the living room and watch TV. There's nothing on but old *Star Trek* episodes. We turn down the volume and make up the dialogue, something we do on our most desperate Saturdays. Sally isn't crazy about it, but it still makes her laugh. It feels odd doing it at my house, though. Without Sally.

When we get hungry for lunch, I check to see if "the ladies" really did leave us any doughnuts, but all I find is a tiny bit of cold coffee left in the pot and an empty doughnut box on the counter with a few sprinkles and some jelly smudges left on the wax paper inside. I make us some lemonade from a mix and we eat an entire bag of low-fat, gourmet potato chips instead.

"I feel ill," Henry says. He turns the bag over and studies the ingredients. "No trans fats!" he says.

"Yay."

We put our glasses in the kitchen sink and wash the chip grease off our hands.

"I bet Claire bought those chips," I say. "We've never had them before."

"Think she'll be mad at us for eating them all?"

"She's been basically living here for a week. I think the least she can do is donate a bag of chips."

"True. So, now what?"

"Come on," I say. "Let's go to the roof."

"The roof?"

"Yeah. You'll see."

Upstairs in the bathroom, I have to struggle to get the screen open. There's a dead spider on the sill. I reach through the frame and pull myself up and out. The surface of the shingles digs into my bare knees when I turn back to help pull Henry through.

I crawl to the place where I sat next to my mom, right under a leafy branch. I lean back against the slanted roof. Henry leans back next to me. We look up at the bright green leaves. The sunlight sparkles through them like holes in lace. It feels good to have Henry breathing quietly at my side. Just being here. I don't want to think about my mom and Claire dragging Sally around to all the mall stores. I don't want to worry about whether they will know to take her in the plus-size stores. Or if they will force her to sit at the makeup counter and have a facial with them. The whole situation makes me feel uneasy. Like Sally is their new project and not their new friend.

"What are you thinking about?" Henry asks.

I'm sure he won't want to know, so I just sigh. "Nothing," I say.

"Yeah, me too. I like it up here. It's peaceful."

I turn my head so I can watch him look up at the green lace above us. At the same time, he turns to face me, too. When our eyes meet, I feel butterflies in the pit of my stomach. I don't dare move. I don't dare think about what they mean.

When we were eight, Henry kissed me while we were playing with his Star Wars figures. We were making C-3PO and R2-D2 argue about rescuing Anakin when he paused and kissed me right on the lips. I yelled "Hey!" and pushed him away. His face turned red and sweaty, and he pretended it didn't happen.

I know it's crazy, but suddenly I want him to try again. I want him to take my hand in his warm, soft one.

"Henry," I start. But I don't know what to say. I don't know what to ask for.

We look at each other for a split second longer, then he turns to face the leaves.

I will my heart to slow down and concentrate on the warm shingles against my back. I listen to the traffic going up and down the street, the birds arguing over their spaces, the squirrels chattering about a found nut. This was supposed to be my escape place. Not my "bring your best friend and want him to kiss you" place. And since he's not making attempts to move any closer, maybe it isn't.

I imagine my mom up here in this exact same spot when she was my age, wanting to run away. I imagine her standing at the window after she got pregnant, and not coming back out, trapped inside the house. And then I imagine her here the other night. Sitting in the fading light. Alone. And I'm glad I brought Henry here after all, because I never want to look like that.

Henry's eyes are closed but he's tapping his fingers at his side.

"Do you ever wonder why our moms never tried to find someone new?" I ask.

"Sometimes," he said. "I mean, when I was really little I used to wonder if I'd get a new dad. I didn't really want one—" He pauses, as if he's realized something. Then he sits up and looks at me with his worried face.

"I think I told her that. I think I told her that I didn't want another dad."

"There's nothing wrong with saying that. You were a kid."

But he doesn't seem sure. "Do you think she's been alone all this time because of me?"

What I think is that it would probably take more than just wanting a man in her life for Sally to get one. Which is horrible of me. So I think hard for a better answer. I think of Sally in that small house all those years, never leaving. Never really living, except through her soaps. Alone, just like my mom.

"It's not your fault, Hen," I finally say. "I think maybe Sally was just afraid. Maybe she was afraid of getting hurt again, you know? I mean, maybe it was just safer to live through the soaps, where everything eventually turns out okay, more or less."

"Yeah," he says. "I guess so. Do you think that's why your mom never dated, too? Why she never left home? Because she was afraid?"

I remember all the times my mom came home late at night after work and how I never really knew who she was with. She always told Gus she'd been out with friends from Lou's. But the only time she ever mentioned anything about dating was to say she was too tired to date. And who had time. But maybe that was just an excuse. Maybe she was too scared, just like Sally.

"Maybe," I say. And I realize how sad that is. And how I really don't know my mom at all. "I guess I shouldn't have been so hard on her last night. She was only trying to protect me."

"Nah. I think she went a little nuts." He leans back and closes his eyes. "Man, our moms are really messed up." His voice sounds a little shaky, like he's trying not to cry.

I lean next to him and slowly, very slowly, reach my hand across the rough shingles until I find his. He doesn't say anything as our fingers meet.

"I don't want to be lonely and scared like them," I say.

He squeezes my hand. I wish I could tell if it's a friendly squeeze or something more.

"You won't be," he says. "I promise."

chapter sixteen

Our hands don't even have time to get sweaty before the familiar sound of ABBA playing on a car stereo comes from the street below. Henry lets go and starts to sit up.

"Let's just stay," I say. "I don't want to deal with them."

He leans back down and covers his eyes with his arm. Car doors creak open and slam shut. Then my mom's keys jiggle in the lock of the trunk and there's the rustle of what sounds like twenty shopping bags being hauled out of it.

We listen to their mumbled voices inside. "Bean?" My mom calls from downstairs.

I don't answer.

Someone opens my mom's tiny dormer window above us. Then springs on her bed squeak. "Lord, it's hot," Claire's voice says through the screen.

"I'll make lemonade," my mom says. Her flip-flops slap against her feet as she goes down the hall.

Bags rustle in the bedroom.

"This will look great on you," Claire says.

"Oh, I'm not sure," Sally answers.

"Try it on!"

"I don't know."

"Come on, Sally! Live a little. I'll put on my new outfit, too. Too bad Bean and Henry aren't here. We could put on a fashion show for them! Did you ever do that when you were a kid? My sister and I used to put on a show every September when we got home from buying our new school clothes."

Henry jerks his head toward the bathroom window in a "Let's go" sort of way. But I stay put.

"Sally," Claire says a little quietly, "are you worried about Lexie?"

"Why?" Sally says even more quietly.

Yes, I think, turning my head toward the window. *Why?*

"She still hasn't told Bean about us."

I look at Henry.

Us?

"How long do you think this can go on before she figures it out herself? Don't you think we should tell her now?" Claire asks.

My ears start to buzz.

"The truth can hurt," Sally says quietly.

Shopping bags rustle.

I dig my fingernails into the hot shingles.

"But it shouldn't have to. Damn it. We've been quiet for

fifteen years. I want to shout it from the rooftop!" Claire's voice is loud again, as if she really is going to climb out my mom's bedroom window and join us.

I look at Henry, who stares at me with his mouth open. My brain swims in my skull and I can't quite make sense of what's happening. And yet, it *all* makes sense now. It's so obvious.

Henry concentrates on chewing the inside of his mouth. A dribble of sweat trickles down his temple and over his jaw, but he doesn't wipe it away.

"Hey, sweetie." It's my mom's voice. "You going to model for me?"

"Maybe I should go," Sally says.

"Oh, stay," says Claire. "We promise to be good."

Henry and I don't move.

"I was telling Sally I think it's time," Claire says.

"I know, I know," my mom says. "I just don't know how to bring it up. All these years keeping us a secret. How do you just come out and tell your kid you're gay?"

I knew the words were coming, but somehow I'm still not prepared to hear that my mom's been lying to me my entire life. I feel myself slowly slipping down the slanted roof, and Henry's hands grabbing at me. At the same time he yells, "Bean!" and I scream.

Everything happens at high speed. The window screen creaks as someone forces it open. I look up and see my mom's panicked face.

My throat tightens. Henry holds on. His hands are under

my armpits. I feel like a puppet. I cringe, then force myself to turn and face my mom. Her red hair is falling out of its ponytail.

"Why didn't you tell me?" I ask, crawling back up the roof with Henry following carefully behind.

"Beany," she says. Her eyes plead with me, but I'm not sure what they're asking. The shingles scrape my knees and the palms of my hands. Henry crawls beside me, breathing heavily. He puts a hand on my back.

My mom opens her mouth again but nothing comes out.

I'm crying.

Sally's head appears next to my mom. "Hen!" she yells when she sees him. "You'll fall!"

Claire squeezes her head between my mom's and Sally's. They're like the Three Stooges with their heads popping out the window like that—only they are not funny. They are the anti Three Stooges.

"I'm so sorry, Beany," my mom says. She looks scared, but I'm not going to let her make me feel sorry for her. I don't even think she knows what she's apologizing for: being gay or lying. It makes me want to scream.

"You could have told me!" I yell, digging my nails into the hot shingles. "You could've trusted me!"

"It's not your mom's fault, Beany," Claire says, putting her hand on my mom's shoulder.

"Oh, would you SHUT UP, Claire! You don't know anything!" I yell. "I would have understood!" The tears are really flowing now. I want to scream and run and disappear all at the same time. The truth of it floods over me so fast I can hardly breathe.

"Why didn't you tell me?" I sob.

"I was afraid," my mom says. She's crying too. Even Claire looks like she might start. Sally too. Good.

"What were you afraid of?" I ask. "What did you think I would do? Were you just going to lie to me for the rest of my life? Am I that unimportant to you? Do you not know me at all? Do you really think I'd hate you just because you like women? This isn't the 1950s, Mom!"

"Oh, Beany, that's not it at all."

"What then!" My nose is running but I don't dare reach up to wipe it. "I swear, Mom. You don't know me. I'm your daughter and you don't know me."

Henry manages to shift around to a safer position, not facing the three heads.

"Please come in so we can talk."

"Just forget it," I say. "It doesn't matter. Now you guys can stop sneaking around, pretending to be friends."

"We *are* friends," my mom says.

"No you're not! You're *girl*friends! And you're—you're liars! All three of you!"

I twist away from them as the truth continues to sink in. They all lied to me. Even Sally kept the secret. Sally, who has been a part of *my* life all these years. Mine. Not theirs.

"Bean, just come inside. The whole neighborhood can hear you."

"I don't care!" I yell. "Claire's the one who wants to shout it from the rooftop! Now's her chance!"

"That's not fair!" Claire snaps. "Your mom was only trying to protect you."

I turn back to face them. "Protect me from what?"

"The truth!" my mom says. She wipes her eyes. "Oh, Bean. The truth about Gus. And me. And everything."

"I don't need to be protected, Mom."

"You don't understand."

"How could I if you don't even give me a chance?"

My mom bites her bottom lip. "It's not that easy," she says quietly.

"You could have told me. You could have told both of us. Gus would have understood. You never gave him enough credit. You were always so mean to him. You were totally misleading him, dressing up like you did and making him think you were out picking up guys. Why would you do that? He was worried about you and you just rubbed it in his face! How could you?" Sobs come out of me and I can't talk anymore. I bury my face against my knees. Henry touches my arm.

"Please. Just go," I say. I feel so ugly and awful. It hurts to feel his eyes on me.

"I'm not leaving you," he says.

"Bean!" My mom tries again. I put my hands over my ears.

"Leave me alone!"

"Honey, it's not what you think," my mom says desperately. "Please come in so we can talk. So I can explain."

Honey? She's never called me honey in my life. That's Sally's word. It's a word for a mother to call her daughter. And it sounds wrong coming from her mouth.

I shake my head and press my hands over my ears even harder. "Leave. Me. Alone."

"Fine." The screen slides down. Their voices move out of the room, but I can hear Claire and my mom yelling at each other. Good.

"Bean," Henry says.

"I'm sorry, Hen. I just—really need to be alone." I don't dare look at him.

"But—"

"Seriously, Henry. Please." I wipe my eyes on the back of my arm.

"Okay," he says quietly. "I understand. Call me later."

He crawls away from me. I listen to him struggle through the bathroom window, then to the quiet he leaves behind. The lacy light through the tree sparkles on the faded black shingles, as if this should be a magical place. I scoot over to a shadier spot. In the distance, summer traffic keeps moving. Car stereos blare music I can't hear the words to, only feel.

She lied. She lied she lied she lied.

But why?

I ask the question over and over, but I can't think of any

reasons that make sense or don't hurt. She didn't trust me. She didn't know me well enough to know I wouldn't care. She didn't feel close enough to me to want to share the truth.

After a while, the heat from the sun on the shingles is too much to bear, and I carefully crawl back toward the bathroom window and climb through as quietly as I can. Then I drink from the sink faucet. The water tastes metallic and dirty. I put the lid down on the toilet and sit, listening for my mom and Claire. But the house is silent. So silent, I have to cover my ears from the ringing of it.

chapter seventeen

I don't know how she comes up on me, but she's here, on silent feet, standing in the bathroom doorway. Her face is splotchy from crying.

"Let me explain," she says slowly.

"You don't understand," I interrupt. I'm still sitting on the stupid toilet seat lid. It's cold and uncomfortable, but I'm trapped.

"Bean—"

"It's not about you and Claire, Mom. It's about the secrets. The lies. You could have told me. But you never took the time to get to know me well enough to know that. You were always working extra shifts, or staying out late with—Claire."

"It wasn't you I wanted to keep the secret from. It was Gus."

"We aren't—weren't—the same person!"

"Bean. I didn't tell *anyone*." She stays in the doorway, her hands on the frame to hold herself up.

"I'm not *anyone*. I'm your daughter! Don't you get that? I know you never wanted me. But I'm here! Besides, welcome to the twenty-first century, Mom. People are gay. It's not a big deal. Lying about it is!"

She takes a step inside the tiny room. "I didn't want to hurt you, Beany! I didn't want you to have to keep a secret from Gus. He loved you."

"God, Mom. He loved you, too! You know he did."

She rolls her eyes and sits down on the edge of the tub.

"He did," I say again.

"You don't know what you're talking about."

"Yes I do. Gus wasn't the bad guy you make him out to be. Look how he took care of me! He was the best grandfather. And he was probably a great father, too. You just— did stuff to make him upset. You were always wearing those short skirts and stuff just to piss him off. He got angry because he was worried about you! He didn't want you to get hurt again. Like with Bill."

"No. That's not it. That's not why Gus spoke to me like that."

"Yes it is! You're lying again!"

"I wish I was." She scoots along the edge of the tub, closer to me. "God, I really wish I was."

"What is it, Mom. More lies? More secrets you need to come clean on? What, did you lie about Bill, too?"

She clasps and unclasps her hands. She plays with her

thumb ring. She picks the dirt from under the nail of her index finger.

"You did, didn't you? I can't believe this. Why can't you just tell me the truth!"

"The truth hurts. That's why I haven't told you."

"Stop it! Stop with the stupid clichés! I'm not a little kid! Maybe the truth hurts *you*, Mom. But it doesn't hurt me. It's the lies that hurt. *Your* lies. You're acting like you know what's best for me. You don't know anything about me!"

"And you don't know anything about *me*!"

"Yeah! I know! And whose fault is that?" I slap my knees with my hands, getting ready to bolt out of the room.

She rubs her palm over her forehead. "You don't want to know this. Trust me. Some things are better left unknown."

"That's such a cop-out! Why don't you trust me to be able to handle things?"

"Fine! You want to know the truth? You think you're so strong? You think you know everything? Fine. He caught us together, okay?"

"You and Bill?"

"No! Me and—me and Claire."

"We were talking about Bill. I don't care about stupid Claire!"

She looks like she's about to explode. "Do you want to hear this or not? You said you want to know the truth, well, it starts with Claire. And don't you call her stupid ever again!"

"Fine."

"Claire and I were together in my room when Gus walked in on us. We were just holding each other."

I roll my eyes.

"Okay, okay. We were kissing. He—his face turned purple. I thought he was going to have a heart attack. I didn't know what to say. The three of us stood there, frozen. Then Gus finally caught his breath. He screamed at Claire to get out. Claire started to try to talk and he stepped toward her like he was going to beat her. She fled. Then he turned to me. He looked like—" She covers her eyes and shakes her head.

"What?"

She pulls her hands away and looks down at the bathmat. "Like he was seeing a stranger. A stranger he despised. Before I could even try to explain, his hand shot out and hit me so hard I fell to the floor."

I try to imagine Gus doing such a thing and can't. Yes, I saw him slap her that one time. But he would never really hurt her. I know it. "I—I don't believe you. Gus wouldn't do that!"

"He said he was glad my mother was dead so she didn't have to see how sick her daughter was."

"No," I say. "He was probably just surprised. He overreacted."

"He told me that if he ever saw me with Claire again he would pull me out of school and homeschool me. When Claire tried to call, he had our number changed and said if

I told her what it was, he'd get a restraining order from the police."

I shake my head. "This doesn't sound like Gus." Not my Gus.

"You asked for the truth." She plays with her ring again. "Look, I know it's probably hard for you to accept. I watched him raise you like he raised me. He took care of me just the way he cared for you when you were little. Sometimes I'd see how loving he was with you and I'd think maybe I imagined the whole thing. But I didn't, Bean. I didn't."

"No," I say again. "Not Gus. He would never hit anyone." I think of the spiders he saved. The gentle way he tended the tomato plants. How could those hands hurt anyone?

"We're talking in circles, Bean. I don't know how else to convince you."

"Okay, fine. But even if Gus did do all those things. That still doesn't explain Bill."

She turns away from me. "Bill was just revenge. He was a regular at the restaurant and I knew he liked me. One night I agreed to meet him after work. We started kissing and—things got out of control. I was fifteen. I didn't know how to say no. I didn't know I *could* say no. Gus never taught me anything. I didn't have anyone to teach me what to do. How to stay safe."

"So, my dad raped you?"

"Don't say that."

"Why not? It's true, isn't it? That's what you told Gus, right?"

"How did you—?"

"I'm right, aren't I?"

She shakes her head. "Beany, don't do this."

"Don't do what?"

"This."

"I deserve to know the truth about my father!"

"He didn't rape me. I let it happen." She isn't looking at me. She's fixated on the flowery pattern of the shower curtain. "The whole time, I kept thinking, *Are you happy now, Dad? Is this what you wanted?*"

A tear slips down her cheek, followed by another. She shakes her head and wipes it away.

I look down at her recently pedicured toenails. They're painted the same color as her hair. Her feet are tan and would be pretty if it weren't for the bunions she got from having a horrible job that kept her on her feet all day.

"The worst part is," she says more quietly, "I kept going back for more. I don't know who I was punishing more, me or Gus. He wanted me to be straight so badly, well, I sure was! After I was with Bill, I'd go home and Gus would be sitting in that damn chair looking at me like I was trash, like he knew what I'd just been doing. I'd smile at him and think, *Is this what you wanted, you bastard?*

"Bill would meet me after work. We hardly talked. Just

got right to business. I hated it, but each time, I felt like I was getting my revenge. I blocked out Claire. All I felt was hate. Hate for Gus and hate for myself. But then, everything changed."

"Why?"

She looks at me for just a minute, then puts her hands over her face and groans, "I can't do this."

"It's because of me, isn't it? That's when you got pregnant."

"I need a drink."

I lean back on the seat. It always comes back to me.

"Why didn't you just get an abortion?" When I say the word, I can almost feel myself being sucked into sweet oblivion.

"You say it like it's that easy, Bean."

"It would have been! Just think how different things would be if I'd never been born!"

"Don't say that!"

"Why not? Don't tell me you wanted to have a baby."

"No. No, I didn't. Okay? Is that what you want to hear? That I didn't want you? Will that make you feel better about feeling sorry for yourself?"

"Yes!"

"Of course I didn't want to have a baby. I was barely freaking fifteen years old! Would you want to have a baby right now?"

I can barely imagine making out with someone, let alone doing what she did.

"Then why did you have me?"

She shakes her head. "You act like it's so easy to answer. It's complicated. For one thing, my periods have never been regular, so I didn't think much when I missed a couple of months. Then, when I started feeling sick at work, I got scared. I was too embarrassed to buy a pregnancy test. I didn't have anyone to go to for help. I was so ashamed. Finally, I knew I had to tell Bill. I figured he'd at least help me figure out what to do. What a joke."

"Why? What did he do?"

"He freaked out. We were in his truck and when I told him, he went nuts, slamming the steering wheel with his fists. The dashboard. Everything but me. Then he reached in the glove compartment of his truck and pulled out his wedding ring and told me he didn't need another wife and definitely not another baby. He said this wasn't his problem and to get out. Then he drove away, leaving me all alone.

"I walked all the way home that night. I knew I had to go to a doctor to be sure. I knew I was going to have to tell Gus. I knew, walking in the dark, that no one was going to help me. The next morning I finally went to the clinic and had an exam. It was awful. And that's when I found out I was about four months pregnant and it was pretty much too late to do anything about it."

She takes a deep breath and finally looks over at me.

"And then I just waited. Pretty soon, I couldn't hide it anymore. I was afraid Gus would kick me out of the house, so I made up the story about being raped. Gus went nuts, naturally. At first he didn't believe me, but after a while it was obvious I was on my own. No guy was coming around to do the right thing. I think he wanted to believe my story as much as I started to. Needed to. And then I had you and Gus changed a little, I admit. He was so in love with you. He insisted on taking care of you so I could finish school. I would work all day, then go to night school so I didn't have to face all my old friends. I didn't have time for anything else."

"Where was Claire all this time?"

"She wouldn't talk to me, she was so upset about my fling with Bill. As much as I missed her, I figured it was probably best for everyone. But eventually, she started coming by the restaurant again. And, well, we love each other. We always have. So she forgave me."

She takes a deep breath and lets it all out. "That's it. That's the truth. I know it's probably hard for you to take it all in, but that's all of it. I promise."

She breathes in slowly again, like she's trying out a new body, free of extra weight. Her hands are shaking.

I look at the lines on the palms of my own hands, wondering which ones I inherited from her and which from the father I'll never know. Her words echo back to me. *Another wife. Another baby.* I have a brother or sister somewhere.

"I'm sorry I didn't tell you the truth. I should have known you'd be okay with it. You're right. But the more time went by, the bigger the lie felt. And then I got so used to living that way, I just accepted that was how it would always be."

"God, Mom."

She wipes her forehead with the back of her hand again.

"Give me a chance. Please. Give us both a chance."

I'm not sure if by *both* she means the two of us, or her and Claire. But I don't want to think about Claire. I don't want to think about how things will be now, with Claire living with us. With her acting like she belongs here and I don't. I was just the result of some stupid mistake.

At least now I understand why Claire doesn't like me. I'm a daily reminder that my mom was with someone else. I represent the worst time of her life.

A warm breeze comes through the window, blowing my hair across my cheek. My mom leans forward to brush it away, but I lean back and away from her instinctively.

"I have to go find Henry," I say.

"Okay," she says. "Okay."

She moves her legs to the side so I can walk past her. She doesn't try to touch me again. I can feel her eyes on me as I walk away, down the hall. I picture her sitting on the edge of the tub, watching me leave.

As I walk by Gus's closed door, I stop. I try to imagine him saying the things my mom claims. I try to imagine his angry face when he caught her with Claire.

But I can't.

I just can't believe it.

chapter eighteen

The stairs seem steeper. The clock in the hall taller. The old house smells stronger. I step out onto the porch, quietly shutting the screen door behind me. The peepers are already echoing through the early night. *Weep, weep, weep.*

It's dusk and the sky is gray and overcast. The air smells like rain, though the drops haven't started to fall yet.

Weep, weep.

I move forward but stop at the top step of the porch, looking out at the tiny bit of grass that needs to be mowed. Claire's gold Honda Civic is in the driveway.

I make my way down the steps and along the cracked pavement. As I walk down the sidewalk, I avoid stepping on the cracks.

A car comes along and slows down. I walk faster.

"Hey, girl," a voice says.

I look, even though I know I shouldn't.

The first thing I see is a muscular, tan arm hanging out the window. The face is tan, too. Dirty blond hair and big teeth.

I look away. Just a few more houses and I'll reach Henry's.

"Wanna go to a party?"

I shake my head.

"Aw, come on!"

My cheeks burn. I shake harder.

He revs the engine a bit.

Weep.

"Pleeeeease?"

I look straight ahead. "I have plans," I say quietly.

Why am I crying?

I run.

He speeds up.

"Hey!" he calls. "I didn't mean to scare you!"

I shake my head again and keep running.

"*Freak!*" He speeds up and leaves me behind. Small drops of rain touch the sidewalk. They make a polka-dot pattern on the street.

I wipe my eyes but the tears keep coming.

Up ahead, I see Henry's small house. It's a ranch-style house built on the site where one of the old, painted ladies burned to the ground. It sits between two larger Victorians, like a sad unwanted child. Mr. Clancy, who likes cats, has a house on one side, and Ms. Bea, who hates them, is on the other. The red tip of her cigarette glows in the wet dark of her porch as she watches me hurry to Henry's.

I run up the crumbling brick path to the front door and hesitate. In the past, I always gave a few quick, happy knocks. But tonight, when I step up to the door, it feels different. I feel different.

I knock once and wait.

Heavy footsteps hurry to the door, which opens to Sally's thoughtful, cheerful, "you okay hon?" face.

"Hi," I say. I cry harder. My body shakes. I didn't realize how scared I was until the door to safety opened.

"Sweetie." Sally makes a sad face to mirror mine. "Aw, sweetie."

She opens her large arms and I lean into her. They wrap around me and hold me up. Her polyester rose blouse smells like real roses and a hint of talcum powder. And maybe under that, a little sweat. Sally.

"Ah, girl. It's okay," she says into my hair.

I know she thinks I'm upset for all the wrong reasons, but I don't have the energy to correct her. I just want her big, soft arms around me.

"I'm all right, really," I say, when I finally pull away from her. "I'm just—glad to be here."

I wipe my eyes dry with the palm of my hand.

"Is Henry here?"

"Of course. He's in his room." She makes a cautious sort of face. "Beany, honey. You know your mom is in love, don't you?"

Oh, brother.

"I know, Sally."

"She was just trying to protect you, honey. Sometimes people do crazy things to protect the ones they love. Sometimes they do the wrong things."

I have the keen sense that Sally is quoting from a recent episode of *Days*.

I nod. I can feel Sally loving me in a way I've never felt before and I instantly forgive her for keeping the secret. It doesn't even seem to matter anymore. She looks changed to me, standing there in the hallway instead of sitting on her couch. She seems happier.

The house smells like fresh-popped popcorn. As I pass through the tiny living room to get to Henry's room, I notice the familiar metal mixing bowl on the coffee table. It's full of popcorn instead of the usual Doritos.

I walk down the hallway, passing a series of framed school photos of Henry—one per grade. His hair never changes. The background is always the same sky blue. Henry's pudgy elbow rests on the same stupid fake wood fence, his chin held expertly in his hand. He fake smiles at me year after year, until I reach the end of the hallway.

His bedroom door is closed, so I knock.

"Yeah?" he asks.

"It's me," I say through the particle-board door.

"Oh. Uh, it's open."

I turn the knob slowly. He's sitting on his bed with his Frank Lloyd Wright architect book open on his lap. He always looks at it when he's upset. He says the photos calm him.

"Hi," I say.

He closes the book and sits up a bit.

"Hey."

I step inside his immaculate bedroom. The walls are wood panel, which he hates. The floor is covered with dusty blue carpet, which he also hates. His comforter matches. There aren't any posters on the walls, just an Ansel Adams calendar. Henry likes spareness. Sometimes I catch him cringing just looking at the porcelain knick-knacks Sally has on every available surface in the rest of the house.

"You okay?" he asks.

"Yeah," I say, wondering if he can tell I've been crying. I've shut the door behind me but I swear I hear Sally's footsteps creaking down the hall.

"You sure?"

I sit on the edge of his bed and stare at my hands. They're still shaking.

"I'm all right."

"What happened after I left?"

"My mom and I talked. She told me the truth. About everything."

He shifts on his bed to make more room for me.

I slide back and lean against the paneled wall. "She told me the truth about my dad."

"Oh."

"He didn't rape her. It was a lie to keep Gus off her back about Claire."

"I'm so confused."

"Before the Bill incident, Gus caught my mom and Claire—you know—together. My mom said he totally freaked out and forbade my mom to see Claire again. So then she decided she'd show him by having an affair with some older guy. Maybe she was also trying to prove to herself she wasn't gay or—who knows. Anyway, she wound up getting pregnant. She thought Bill would take her away or something. But he freaked out when she told him. Turns out he was married and already had a new baby!"

"Whoa!"

"Yeah. I know. It's so *Days*."

There's a noise in the hallway.

Henry rolls his eyes. "Spy," he mouths.

But I don't mind if Sally hears.

"Anyway, by the time my mom found out Bill wasn't going to stay with her, it was too late to have an abortion. So she made up the story about being raped by some stranger in the parking lot so Gus wouldn't kick her out of the house."

"That is the most messed-up story I ever heard."

"I know. It's even more messed up than *Days*."

He smirks. "Totally. So, what happened to Bill?"

"I dunno. Some of the other customers who knew him told her he'd left his wife and baby and everything. Just disappeared." I sigh. "Great dad story I have, isn't it? He deserted not just one baby, but two."

There's another sound in the hallway. A human sound. Like a choke. And then footsteps running down the hall.

Henry jumps to his feet. "Mom?" He runs to the door and down the hall, leaving me alone. "Mom!"

I race to the living room. Sally is lying on the floor, sobbing. Henry is on his knees, bent over her.

"Mom!" he says. "What is it?"

Sally doesn't answer, just sobs and sobs into the carpet. Her huge body heaves up and down. I've never seen Henry hug Sally before but now he's hunched over her, holding her.

"What is it?" he keeps saying.

"William," she finally manages. "My William!"

Henry turns to me but I don't know what to do.

"Who's William?" Henry asks quietly.

Sally sobs louder.

"Your father's name!" she wails. It was William! Bill!"

Henry's face falls. Sally always refused to tell Henry anything about his dad. She said it was too painful and that they had to move on.

Henry looks at me, confused. I feel my mouth hanging open. I shake my head.

No.

That's all I can think.

No. Impossible.

Sally lifts her face to Henry. Her mascara is smudged

all down her cheeks. Large streaks of hair have fallen out of the bunnish thing she has it in. They're soggy with tears. I've seen Sally cry over her soaps plenty of times, but nothing like this.

Henry turns from me, to Sally, and back to me. His mouth hangs open, too. And I know what he's thinking. What it means if our dads are the same person. My heart twists in my chest.

"It couldn't be," I say.

Sally sobs harder and hides her face in Henry's neck.

"It's just a coincidence!" I'm crying now, too. Almost choking.

Henry looks at me helplessly as he tries to hold Sally's head up.

"I have to go," I say. Fear rises up in my throat, and I know I'm going to throw up. "I have to go."

I leave them there, on the floor, and run.

chapter nineteen

It's pouring rain out, and dark. My flip-flops squish as I run through the wet, stepping in puddles. I slip and the plastic cuts between my toes. I kick them off and run barefoot until I reach my house.

The lights are on in the kitchen but nowhere else. I wait on the porch to catch my breath, then sneak inside and upstairs.

I don't look at Gus's door as I pass. I head straight for the bathroom, the window, the roof.

The asphalt shingles dig into my bare knees as I crawl to my mom's spot. The rain is lighter under the leaves, but it still drips down on me, mixing with my own tears.

They're wrong. It's ridiculous! This isn't a soap opera. Things like this don't happen in real life!

But the look on their faces makes it feel real. And if it is, then it all comes back to me again. If I didn't exist, every-thing would be better. If I'd never been born, they'd be a happy family. Henry would know how to fish. Sally would have her perfect man. My mom would have graduated from high school, gone to college, and escaped. Gus could have lived in peace.

If I'd never been born, everyone I know would be better off. I'm not feeling sorry for myself. It's just a fact.

I imagine Henry and his dad fishing happily while Sally sits in the bow of their own rowboat. They are a family. I imagine my mom going to college and getting together with Claire in some other state, far away from Gus. I imagine Gus living in the house. Alone, but content to be that way. Maybe he would have friends over to play cards and share his wine with. Maybe the whole end of his life wouldn't have been spent fighting with my mom and helping to take care of me.

I lean back on the roof, letting the wet shingles seep through my shirt.

There's thunder in the distance and a shock of lightning far off. I can't remember the rule for counting and figuring out how far away the storm is. I will it to come closer and blast me.

The rain slips down the roof and pools around me, cold and soaking. My head aches. A crack of thunder claps again. Louder. The rain gets stronger. I slide a few inches down the slippery shingles. The darkness below me looks bottomless. If I just pick up my legs and let myself slip . . .

"Beany!" My mom's voice is louder than the thunder. "What the hell are you doing out there!" She's halfway out the bathroom window, squinting at me as the rain splatters.

I don't move. I don't acknowledge her. I just peer down at the inviting darkness.

"Beany!" she yells again.

I look up at the leaves on the tree—small, dark hands blocking out the sky.

"Bean, you get in here right now! You'll get electrocuted!"

I turn away from her. For the first time in my life, I know where the word *heartache* comes from. Everything hurts. Everything's wrong. Who cares if I get electrocuted? They'll all be better off if I simply let myself slip down over the side of the roof into the nothing.

There's a rustling and a "hummph" as my mom heaves herself through the window.

"Stay away!" I yell through the rain.

"Come inside!"

"No! You left this place to me, remember?"

"I didn't mean when it's pouring rain and *thunder and lightning*, for Christ's sake!" She pulls herself out the rest of the way and crawls across the roof.

"Are you crying?" she asks.

I wipe my face. "It's the rain," I lie.

"Oh, Beany," she says quietly. "I'm sorry I didn't tell you sooner. You're right. I should have told you a long time ago. No excuses, okay? I was wrong." We look at each other in the dark. I don't even know where to start now.

How to tell her what's happened. How there's so much more now to be sad about. To regret. So I just shake my head over and over, as if I'm saying no to everything in my life.

"Pearl," she almost whispers.

"What?"

"Pearl," she says again, staring at me.

"No," I say. "I'm no pearl."

It could be the rain, but deep down I know there are tears mixed in the raindrops covering her face, too.

"Yes," she says.

I wish I wasn't crying. I wish I could look at her and say I'll leave for her. I'll leave so she and Claire can have a happy life at last.

She grasps my shoulder and squeezes.

"Pearl," she says again.

"Why are you calling me that?"

"To remind you."

I wipe the wet from my eyes. "Of what?"

Her hand moves from my shoulder to my back. It feels warm and strong and unfamiliar. "Do you know why I named you that?"

I shake my head. I always hated my name. Both names, really.

"When I held you for the first time and looked into your face, all my feelings about you changed. I'd thought of you as a mistake. A burden. Something that would ruin my life forever."

"Are you supposed to be making me feel better?"

"I know you appreciate honesty, so I'm giving it to you, okay? Anyway, all those feelings went away when I held you. I was terrified of you, but I could also see how special you were. This living thing. In my arms! It was like all this bad stuff I'd held inside turned into something beautiful. Your grandmother always loved pearls. She said they were one of nature's miracles. I remember when I was really little I'd sit in her lap and touch her earrings, and she'd explain how pearls were made. And I guess, when I saw you, I felt like I'd made a miracle too.

I touch my earrings.

"Gus hated the name, of course. He was so disgusted with me still, he didn't want any reminders of Mom associated with the things that I'd done. But when he held you that first time, he broke down in tears. I promise you I saw his hate toward me melt away, even if it wasn't forever. When he looked at your sweet face, I saw love seep back inside him. I saw it in his eyes and the way his whole body softened. He loved you so much. I know you have a hard time believing it, but I love you, too."

She tries to squeeze my shoulder again, but her arm around me feels awkward. She still doesn't know how to touch me. How to hold me. How to be my mother.

I want to hate her for being so stupid. For not knowing how to love her own kid.

But I don't.

"So, Gus called me Bean because he hated my real name," I say. "But what about you?"

"Oh, I tried to call you Pearl for a while, but the fatter and cuter you got, the more Bean seemed a better choice. We called you Little Bean. For the first few months, it seemed like you kept the peace between us. But then I went back to work and Gus wanted to know where I was every minute. And pretty soon we were back to the same old battles."

The tree above cries raindrops on us as we sit quietly.

I close my eyes and think of Henry and Sally and what they must be doing right now. I imagine them sitting on the floor, holding each other in their grief. Maybe wishing they never knew me.

I face my mother, realizing she is the one with all the answers. She stares out into the dark with a distant look on her face.

"Mom," I say, "tell me more about Bill."

chapter twenty

We make a deal that if I follow her inside, she'll tell me more.

"He was tall, with thin hair," she says as she rubs her hair dry with a towel in the bathroom. I hold a towel wrapped around me. The bathroom floor is soaked.

"Those aren't really the details I was hoping for," I say.

She elbows me like a friend sharing secrets would. "I know. C'mon."

I follow her to her bedroom. I don't know the last time I was in here. It's more purple than I remember. It feels more like a teenager's room than a mom's. There's a photo of her and Claire on her dresser. It looks like they took it at the mall when they were shopping with Sally. They look so happy they're practically glowing.

"Come sit," she says, patting the bed. We sit cross-legged, facing each other. The bedspread is a silky purple.

I never thought of my mom as wanting to be surrounded by so many girlish colors. It's like a rainbow in here.

"Okay," she says. "What do you want to know?"

"I guess I do want to know more about what he looked like. I mean, did he look at all like—" *Henry,* I want to ask. But I can't get my mouth around the name.

"He wasn't much to look at." She uncrosses her newly tanned legs and stretches them out beside me. "He was average, I guess. Brown hair. Brown eyes. I thought he was all right at the time. But . . . I don't know, Beany. I thought these weren't the kinds of details you wanted."

"I know. It's just—" Henry's eyes are brown. Sally's eyes are brown. I wish I could remember that Mendel's law thing for determining eye color. "I was just wondering if he looked like me." Or Henry.

She looks at me, squinting her eyes in the dull bedroom light, as if she's looking for traces of him in me. "Well, you're a lot prettier, I know that. I'm sorry, I don't remember the specifics. It was usually dark." She half laughs.

"Yeah. That's funny," I say.

"Oh, come on, Bean. Lighten up."

"Lighten up? Are you serious?"

"What?"

I shake my head and get off her stupid purple comforter.

"I shouldn't be here! I should never have been born! Gus is dead! He's the only person who really loved me! My life sucks! And it's—" The photo of her and Claire catches my eye. It isn't my fault. It's hers. "It's all your fault! You and—and *Claire*! You never cared about me! You never cared about the other person Bill left! Or his kid! All you cared about was hurting Gus and sneaking around with Claire!"

"What? What are you talking about!"

"Never mind! I don't know why I even try to talk to you! You're just a selfish, crazy . . . I don't know!"

I stomp out of the room and down the hall. I'm about to go into my own room but instead I open Gus's door, step inside the room, and slam the door shut.

Her footsteps slap down the hall.

"Pearl Collatti, open this door!" She bangs on my bedroom door, not realizing I'm not there.

Stupid.

I have the dumbest mom on the planet.

"What's going on up there?" Claire yells.

Across the room I see my reflection in Gus's mirror. I creep closer and stare at myself, looking for a trace of Henry. Are my eyes like his? My nose? Ears? Mouth? No. Nothing. There's nothing.

"Open this door right now!" My mom yells across the hall.

I roll my eyes.

My bedroom door rattles, then creaks open.

"Bean? She's not in there."

"Where is she?" Claire asks.

"I don't know, obviously."

I get on the floor and hide under Gus's bed just in case they figure out where I've gone.

It smells dusty. Dusty and empty.

I lie on my back and stare at the coils in the box spring above. A cobweb hangs over me, abandoned and forgotten.

Whispers sneak under the door. I hold my breath even though I'm not sure why I'm hiding anymore.

"Just leave her alone for a bit. She's freaked out."

"She's my daughter. I should at least try to talk to her."

"You did try! She's just not ready. C'mon, honey. Let's go to bed."

"But I don't know where she is!"

"She's a big girl. She can take care of herself. She's probably at Sally's."

Nice Claire. She probably hopes I'll run away.

Their footsteps and voices fade down the hall.

I lie there for what must be an hour, breathing in the dust. The smell of lost days. My back aches against the hardwood floor. When I can't take it anymore, I carefully roll out from under the bed and cross the room on silent feet.

I open the door and stick my head into the hallway. There's a light coming from my mom's room, but I'm sure they're not waiting up to see if I make it home safely from wherever I could be.

I go into my room and crawl into bed. But I can't sleep.

The situation is beyond *Days of Our Lives.* All we need is for Gus to show up at the door and say, "Surprise! I'm not really dead!" And then Bill will come walking in and say that he's back and wants us all to be one big happy family. Even Claire. I can almost hear the hourglass theme music in the background.

Outside, the peepers sing incessantly as the rain continues to pour. It's past one in the morning. There are mumblings through the wall that separates me and my mom. And Claire. I turn on my side and put my pillow over my head so I don't have to listen.

chapter twenty-one

I'm drenched in sweat when I wake up the next morning. I sit up and eye the phone next to my bed. The numbers are automatic. I know the sequence of tones so well that as I press each button I can hum it like a song. I expect Sally's usual pickup on the second ring. Sally always waits for the phone to ring twice. She says one ring makes her seem too eager, but three is rude.

After the fifth ring, their voice mail picks up. I didn't even know they had voice mail. An electronic-sounding woman's voice comes on and tells me to leave a message. I hang up and redial in case I got the number wrong after all. I dial more slowly. The song sounds sadder this way.

I get a machine again.

"Hello?" I say nervously. "It's, um, Bean. Henry? Could you call me back if you get this message? Thanks."

I hang up and watch the phone.

I imagine Henry sitting on his bed, staring at his ceiling

and hearing my voice come through the unused answering machine. Hating me.

Then I imagine Sally bursting into tears at the sound of my voice, and immediately wish I hadn't left a message.

I go downstairs and open the freezer in search of a mini Snickers, then remember Henry and I already finished the bag. I stand in front of the open freezer door and let the cold mist touch my face. It could swallow me. When I grab the bag of coffee beans, I notice a new bag of Snickers hidden behind a Ben & Jerry's frozen yogurt container.

I take the beans and the bag from the freezer and start a pot of coffee. While I wait for the coffee to brew, I take two bars from the bag and put the rest back in the freezer. The coffee sputters into the pot slowly, then begins to drip. I watch it while the hole in my chest aches to the drips. The two Snickers sit on the table like happy friends. Everything around me is in twos. Two clean coffee mugs in the dish drainer. Two dish towels hanging neatly folded over the oven door handle. Two dirty wineglasses next to the sink.

There's no room for three here.

As soon as the coffee's done, I pour myself a mug, grab the Snickers, and head for the front porch. I sit on the steps and dunk the first bar into the coffee until the chocolate is drippy, then lick the melted coating off it. The birds are singing all around me. The morning traffic is heading for work. I look down the street in the direction of Henry and

Sally's house. Weeds grow in the cracks in the sidewalk. Puddles from last night's rain darken the dips in the pavement, and sad little worms who've come out for a drink, or whatever it is they feel the need to do when it rains, lie stranded in the hot morning sun, not sure how to get back to where they came from.

My feet are pointing in Henry and Sally's direction. But my body says *stay.*

I eat the naked Snickers. It doesn't taste as good without the chocolate on it.

The coffee is too hot to sip properly so I set it down.

A crow caws from the direction of the carriage house. The door is open, like a mouth calling me over to it. I leave my coffee on the top step.

There are certain smells that throw you back to a memory, like mothballs, or turpentine, or alcohol on your mom's breath. The smell of the garage is Gus's smell. Of fishing memories. The smell of dirty water and fiberglass rowboats and musty life jackets and wooden oars that creak.

Gus. Gus. What would you say about all of this? What would you do?

I find the key on the hook and leave the familiar smells.

When I get to the dock, I imagine Gus coming here by himself. Methodically unlocking the boat, putting the oars in their slots, pushing away from the dock. Drifting away from shore. Alone. The water smells stagnant even though there's a light breeze blowing across the surface. Another familiar smell that brings me back to days with Gus. Days when I was too young to know I was smelling filth.

I fit my hands over the ends of the oars and row. I remember leaning over the side of the boat when I was little, watching the swirls the oars made as Gus rowed. We called them water tornadoes. I stop rowing and feel the boat silently glide across the water. I never understood what Gus got out of coming out here until now. Now, I can breathe the peace, even if it smells like the Dumpster at Lou's. There's something calming about being out here all alone while the world keeps going without a thought about you.

I lift my face to the sun and relax my grip on the oars, wondering how far I'd go if I kept drifting and let the current carry me away. When the sun starts to burn my face, I sit up and peer into the water. There are no answers down there. There's no Gus. He can't tell me what he got out of coming out here day after day trying to escape the lies of his life, just like my mom tried to escape the truth by hiding on the roof. There's only so long you can try to escape before there's nothing left to escape from, because you've lost it all. After a while it must be like escaping from nothing to nothing.

I hold the oars tight as the boat rocks gently. I'm not going to be like them. The only real way to escape is to face the truth, whatever it is. Maybe they never left this place because they never knew how to deal with what was real. It's like their own lies kept them stuck here. I start rowing. I turn the boat around and row against the current. Past all the familiar run-down houses that seem full of hopelessness, as if their hope has been swept slowly away by the current. But I'm not going to be. When I leave, it's going to be on my own two feet.

Back at the dock, I grab hold of the post and step out, but when I do, the rope slips out of my hand and the boat starts to drift away. I get down on my belly and reach for the rope in the water but I can't quite get it. I curse at myself for being so stupid. I will not give up now that I've finally started to feel motivated for the first time in my life. I lean farther out and practically fall in. Just as my fingers curl around the slimy rope, a hairy, dark arm with an American flag tattoo appears next to mine and pulls me back up. He smells like sweat and next-day beer breath like my mom used to have when she still came into my room to wake me up in the morning for school.

I don't want to turn around and see the face that goes with it. But there are some things you can't avoid.

It's Mr. Clancy, Henry's next-door neighbor. The cat man.

"This boat doesn't belong to you," he says.

His hair is peppery gray and his face is leathery, speckled with pointy gray hairs poking out of his jaw and chin.

"Yes it does," I say as I catch my balance. He doesn't look threatening, but he doesn't look exactly harmless.

"This is Gus's boat," he says.

"I know. He's my grandfather. Was. I mean, is. I mean— you knew Gus?"

He nods and leans closer to me, looking more carefully at my face as if he's trying to find Gus in it. "Sorry for your loss, then. You take good care of this boat."

He helps me lock it back up, then turns and starts up the path to the street. He's a skinny old man, and his pants are baggy. I'm not sure how they stay up. The back of his shirt is covered with cat hair. He walks slowly. I want to follow and ask him about Gus, but I don't know how to start. So I fall back a bit and follow at a distance, watching him walk down the sidewalk until he passes my house. One more piece of Gus I didn't know.

When I get home, the house seems very still, as though it's sleeping. My coffee cup is still on the steps. I pick it up and go inside to find my mom.

chapter twenty-two

In the kitchen, I wash my coffee mug and put it in the dish drainer.

"What happened at Sally's last night?"

I spin around. My mom is standing in the doorway of the kitchen. Her baby-doll nightgown is too close to being see-through. The space between her eyes crinkles.

To avoid her gaze, I look down at her feet. She has on her stupid Peds with the pink pompoms on the heel.

"Why?" I ask.

"I just tried to call her. We're supposed to go to the mall. As I was leaving a message on her machine, she picked up and told me to never call her again."

I freeze.

"Did she say why?"

"No she did not, but I'm guessing it has something to do with what happened last night, with why you were so upset."

My cheeks prickle. I lean against the kitchen sink. The wet edge of the counter soaks through the back of my shirt.

"Beany," my mom says, not coming any closer.

"Who was Bill?" I ask.

"What?"

"My father."

"This again? What does he have to do with Sally?"

She shifts her weight from one foot to the other.

"Bill was married," I say.

"I know that! Are you going to try to make me feel guilty again? What does this have to do with Sally?" But she puts her right hand on the doorjamb to steady herself, as if it's dawning on her.

"His wife had a baby. That's what you said."

She reaches out with her left hand to steady herself some more.

"What does this mean?" she asks.

"You tell me, Mom."

"We're supposed to go to the mall."

Claire comes up behind her. "What's going on?"

I stay leaning against the kitchen sink. My mom stays braced in the doorway.

"It's impossible," my mom says, shaking her head. But she looks scared.

"Where did he live?" I ask quietly.

"I don't know!"

"How could you not know? You were sleeping with him! Do you even know his last name?"

"Don't you dare! Don't you dare!" she yells.

"Dare what? Make you feel like a—"

"Don't you dare say that word!"

"Is someone going to tell me what the hell is going on?" Claire asks.

"Nothing!" My mom glares at me. "It's a misunderstanding," she says, letting go of the doorjamb. She slides her feet together and stands up straight to make room for Claire in the doorway. A barricade of crazy. "Of course it is," she adds. Then she laughs in a maniacal way.

"Then why was Sally so upset?" I ask. "Why was she so sure?"

"I don't know! But it has to be a misunderstanding. I mean, it *has* to. What did you tell her, anyway?"

"Nothing! I told Henry what you told me last night. About why Bill left." I eye Claire, unsure how much she knows about my mom's past when it comes to Bill. "We were in Henry's room, but Sally was listening behind the door and then she freaked out."

My mom tilts her head, like she's trying to put all the pieces of the scene together in her mind.

Claire just looks confused.

"Okay," my mom says. "I'm going over there right now to straighten this out."

"Mom!" I yell, finally pulling myself away from the sink. "You can't!"

"Oh yes I can!"

"You're going to upset her even more!" I'm crying again,

imagining poor Sally being confronted by my crazed mom. "You don't understand. She was devastated! You don't know her like I do. Let me go instead."

"She's my friend too," my mom says, as if she's ten. "I'm the one she's upset with. I'm the one who needs to make it right."

"Will someone please tell me what the hell is going on?" Claire asks.

But my mom is already padding down the hall and shoving her waitress shoes on.

Claire glares at me as if it's all my fault that my mom has completely lost her mind.

"Honey!" she calls after my mom. "You can't go outside in your nighty!"

"I know that!" my mom snaps. She changes direction and heads up the stairs.

I race to the phone to try to call Henry again. The machine clicks on. At the beep, I take a deep breath and try to steady my voice so they won't know I'm crying.

"Um," I say, wondering if my voice is filling their tiny living room. "It's me. Please pick up." I wait, imagining Henry and Sally sitting on the couch together without me in my usual spot. I imagine them watching my empty space while they listen to me.

"I think there's been a misunderstanding," I add. "About Bill."

I hate saying his name again. I can almost feel them cringe when I say it. "Please. I'm sure this is just a crazy

165

coincidence. I'm sure! Please pick up." I wait. "Okay. Well, I think my mom is going to try to come over there. I just thought you should know."

I wait a few more seconds, then hang up and stand alone in the kitchen.

When my mom comes downstairs, Claire trailing behind, she looks unstoppable. But at least she's not wearing her nightgown anymore.

"You can't go," I say. "She doesn't want to see you."

"That's why I have to go," she says back, brushing past me.

I follow her onto the porch and down the front steps.

"Maybe Beany's right, Lex," Claire says, following her down the walkway.

"Mom!" I call. "You're going to make things worse! You're only going to hurt her more! She doesn't want to see you!"

She keeps walking. We chase after her. It feels very odd to be on Claire's team.

At Henry's house, my mom begins to march up the walkway to their front door. I start to follow but Claire holds my arm.

"Maybe we should let her go. When she's determined, there's really no stopping her."

"No!" I wrench my arm away. "She's hurt Sally enough. She's going to make it even worse!"

"How has she hurt them? She hasn't done anything! Your mom is the best thing that ever happened to Sally!"

"What!? God, Claire, are you serious? Sally was happy before you two started forcing her out of the house. Getting her drunk. Dying her hair so she looks like a circus freak. You think that's helped her?"

Claire steps back. "Circus freak? How can you say that!"

"You and my mom have made her into some sort of project. But you don't even know her! I've been going to Sally's almost every day since I was seven. We were happy until you two interfered."

"Maybe you were happy. But Sally wasn't."

"How would you know?" I'm so mad I want to hit her.

Claire's face changes. "She told us."

"What?"

Claire looks at her feet. "She hasn't been happy for a long time, Bean."

I glance at the run-down house. My mom knocking at the door and pushing the doorbell.

"But—" I start to say, but my voice cracks. Because Sally has always been sad. And I've always known it. And even though she looks a little ridiculous now, she also looks happy. Well, she did.

I shake my head. "Everything is so messed up," I say.

"We'll fix it," Claire says. And for the first time, I can actually hear sincerity in her voice.

"But not like this," I say.

She surprises me by nodding. "You're probably right."

I leave her standing on the sidewalk and run up to the house. I hear the ding-dong inside as my mom presses the button over and over, but no footsteps come to the door.

"Mom, let's go! Please!"

She presses again. And again.

"I'm not leaving until we straighten this out," she says. "This is all just a huge misunderstanding and we're going to get to the bottom of it right now."

But at least five minutes go by and nothing happens. Claire paces nervously at the curb.

Finally, I turn around and walk back toward the sidewalk.

"Well?" Claire asks.

"They're not home," I lie.

"Huh?"

I ignore her and walk away. I don't know where I'm going, but I can't watch any more of this train wreck.

At the next corner, I come to the MiniMart. It makes me sad to see the storefront. To see the bike rack Henry and I like to lean against while we eat our treats. I cross the street and lean on the rack. It's warm from the sun. There are never any bikes fastened to it. No one around here rides bikes. I sit down and lean against it just like Henry and I have done a thousand times. I close my eyes and let the sun warm my face while I concentrate on not letting any tears leak out. I want Gus back. I want Henry back. I want so much for everything to be like it was. But then I think of my mom sneaking around with Claire. Too afraid to tell Gus the truth. Too ashamed. And Sally, stuck on the couch with her fake *Days* friends feeding her heart with lies about life and love and living. There are no good times to go back to. And now there are none ahead, either. A tear escapes and slowly runs down my cheek.

"Hey," a voice says.

I open my eyes and see his white tennis shoes. I quickly wipe my face with my hand.

"Your mom's still ringing our doorbell," he says, sitting next to me.

When his arm brushes against mine, I want to lean into him and hold on. But he shifts away so we aren't touching.

"I'm so sorry, Hen. For everything. I—"

"Don't," he says. "You don't have to say anything."

"But my mom. She's nuts. I tried to stop her but she wouldn't listen."

He moves his hand as if he's going to put it on my knee, but midway he pulls it back and tries to rub out a dark mark on his sneaker, as if that was the plan all along.

"Sally's gone a little nuts, too. She won't come out of her room."

I shake my head. "This is awful."

"Yeah."

We sit there for a while, watching the usuals go in and out of the store.

"You don't really think it's possible, do you?" Henry finally asks.

I don't dare look at him, for fear I'll see some family resemblance that's been there all along.

"It can't be," I say. But I feel how desperate those words are.

"Yeah."

We're quiet again, but every second seems to linger.

"My mom doesn't believe it," I say, still too afraid to look at him. "Either that or she's determined not to."

And then it dawns on me that Sally seems almost too eager *to* believe it. "Oh," I say out loud by mistake.

"What?" Henry asks, sitting up more.

"Uh, nothing."

"Come on."

"It's just that—" I bite my lip.

"What?"

"What if Sally wants to believe it?"

"What? Are you crazy, too?" He stands up like he's going to walk away from me.

"No!" I say, getting up after him. "I don't mean it in a bad way! It's just—"

He turns to me. "Just what?"

"What if she needs to know why he left so badly, she'll believe this, even if it's awful? What if she needs to know it's not her fault that he left? Or yours?"

He keeps his eyes locked with mine. I feel the hurt pass between us.

"I don't know," he says. "I just don't know."

He starts walking back in the direction of our houses.

"Wait for me," I say.

He slows down and we walk side by side without talking.

When we get near his house, we see Claire and my mom sitting on the steps.

"Great," I say. We stop and watch them.

"Why are they still here?" he asks.

"They're waiting." I roll my eyes.

Henry shakes his head. "They don't know my mom. She won't come to the door. It's not like she isn't practiced at staying in the house."

I hate hearing him say that.

I imagine Sally lying in her big red bed with the rose-covered bedspread and pink and red pillows, fretting quietly and hoping they'll leave. She's probably crying. It makes me want to scream at my mom and Claire to leave her alone.

"I guess it's good that your mom wants to try to help," Henry says.

"No it's not! She's not doing this for Sally. She's doing it for herself. She's trying to clear her conscience, that's all."

I'm sure of it now. For the same reason Sally seems to need to have this craziness be true, my mom maybe even more desperately needs it not to be. I don't think she can bear the thought of having ruined one more person's life. I know how it feels.

"We have to find out the truth," I say.

"How?"

"I don't know. But we have to. How much do you know about your dad? Do you have *any* pictures? Or letters? Anything?" He starts to shake his head, but then he stops.

"Wait. The box!"

"What box?"

"My mom keeps a box under her bed. One time I caught her sitting in bed crying and I saw it sticking out from under the sheets. I asked her what was wrong, but she covered up the box and said she was fine. I didn't dare ask her what she was hiding, but I remember the box because it was red. And one time when I was vacuuming her room, I lifted the dust ruffle on her bed and saw the same red box hidden under there."

"Maybe she has a picture of him in there!"

Henry looks back toward the house. Claire and my mom still haven't noticed us. We step back out of sight.

"Do you think you could sneak into her room and get the box?"

"I don't know. I mean, maybe if she was talking to your mom again and they went out—"

"That seems unlikely at the moment."

"Yeah."

"What about when she goes to use the bathroom or something?"

Henry wrinkles his nose.

"Sorry, but when else would she leave her room?"

"Maybe when she's taking a shower? Then she wouldn't hear me with the water running."

"Perfect!"

"Okay."

"And I'll try to get more out of my mom, if she ever stops stalking your front door."

"Right."

He starts to go, but I grab his arm. "Hen, it's not going to be true. It's not."

He steps out of my reach. "I'll call you later," he says quietly.

I nod, lifting my discarded hand to put a nonexistent strand of hair behind my ear. "I'll try to get them to come home."

We start forward again.

"How did you get past them, anyway?" I ask.

"Back door."

"Ah."

When we get close to the house, he ducks into the neighbor's yard and makes for the back of the house. My mom looks up and sees him. Thankfully, she doesn't follow.

Henry pauses before disappearing around the corner. I wait to see if he'll turn back to face me. But instead he looks at his feet, then slowly steps behind the house.

I take a deep breath and join my mom and Claire.

"You have to leave now," I say.

Claire stands up.

"She's right, Lexie. Just give it up for today." She reaches for my mom's hand and pulls her to her feet.

My mom looks defeated.

"If you're so sure it's not true, help me prove it," I say.

Her eyes meet mine and a look of surprise floods over her. "Of course!" she says, slapping herself on the head. "I have something! I can prove it! Why didn't I think of it before?"

The first answer that comes to mind is *Because you're afraid you can't*, so I keep my mouth shut and lead the way home.

chapter twenty-three

Back home, Claire and my mom are fighting. My mom's bedroom door is shut, but I don't have to press my ear against my own bedroom wall to hear them.

"Why would you have a picture?" Claire yells. "Why on earth would you save a picture?"

"It's not a photograph, it's . . . something else. Something I drew."

"You drew his face? Why? And why would you keep it? My God, Lexie, do I know you?"

"It's not what you think. It's private," my mom cries. "But I need to show Beany."

"Why would you want her to see his face?" I think Claire is crying too. "Why would you ever want her to have anything to do with him? How could you!"

"Stop it!" my mom cries.

"No! I can't stop it! I don't understand you!"

"She's my daughter! I make the decisions!"

"I'm not trying to make decisions for you!"

"You're judging me!"

I put my hands over my ears, but I can't drown out their voices.

Stupid Claire. Who does she think she is, my stepmom?

"You know I drew everything when I was younger. I thought I might find him in my old diary, okay?"

"I would have ripped out those pages!" Claire yells.

"Well, I'm not you!"

I leave my room so I don't have to hear them anymore. In the hallway, I put my hand on the white porcelain doorknob to Gus's room and turn. Inside, the sun shines through the curtains and casts a lacy shadow on the white bedspread. I shut the door and step carefully toward the bed. Instead of lying on it, I crawl under again.

I slowly breathe in the still air. The old wood of the boxspring mattress. The wood polish mixed with dust. I close my eyes and try to block out the fighting, try to focus on the familiar outside noises through the window screen. But I can still hear the muffled noises of my mom and Claire fighting. I can still feel the weight of Henry's sad face, of Sally's tears, pressing against my heart. I close my eyes and breathe in the quiet.

After a while, their voices finally stop. The back of my head aches from being so heavy against the wood floor. I roll over and out from under the bed. Before I open the door, I listen for my mom and Claire. Then, I slowly turn the knob and step into the hallway.

"Hi."

I jump about a mile.

My mom is standing in my bedroom doorway, clutching a familiar-looking notebook in her arms.

"I was just—" I start to say.

"I don't want to know," she interrupts. "Can we talk?"

I nod.

We go into my room and sit on my bed.

"I want you to read this," she says, handing me the notebook. It's a composition notebook, just like the one she gave me for my thirteenth birthday. I look at the cover.

"Is this your diary?"

She nods.

"But that's private," I say, trying to hand it back to her.

She pushes it into my lap. "I know. But I want you to read it anyway."

"Why can't you just tell me what's in it?" I'm so tired of us not being straight with each other. Of hiding. I think of Claire and realize she's the only one who's been brave enough to tell it like it is.

My mom touches the worn cover of the notebook in my

lap. "There are some words—some feelings—that are too hard to speak out loud," she says. "Lots of old ghosts in here I don't want to revisit. But I think it'll answer your questions for good this time. It holds all the truths I have, Bean."

"But—"

"I want you to read it. Please. I think it's the only way you'll really be able to understand what happened back then." She pulls her hand away and rubs it on her thigh, as if she's wiping away any memories that might have seeped out.

"Read it," she says again. "For me." She stands and heads for the door. "Claire, hon, you cleaning up the room?" she calls as she leaves me. "I totally trashed it looking for that thing," she says to me over her shoulder as she walks away.

"In your dreams!" Claire calls back from my mom's room. I guess they aren't fighting anymore.

I touch the book in my hands. I can almost hear it calling to me in my mom's voice. I trace the words on the cover with my finger. The handwriting looks just like mine.

I move my fingers to the edge of the cover, then stop. I know I can't do this alone. I pick up the phone and dial Henry's number. I let the phone ring until the machine answers and hang up, hoping he knows it's me. Then, I wait.

About ten minutes later, the phone rings.

"Hello?"

"Hi," Henry says. His voice is fuzzy.

"Where are you?"

"The pay phone at the MiniMart. I figured that was you who called."

This makes me smile. "Yup. I have something. Can you come over?"

"Uh—"

"What?"

"I'd kind of prefer to avoid your mom."

"Oh. You know I think she's calmed down a bit."

"Still."

"Are you up for another boat ride?"

Henry is already standing at the end of the dock when I get there.

"What'd you find?" he asks. We're both sweating and out of breath.

"A notebook." I hold it up for him to see.

"Um, whose?"

"My mom's. She gave it to me to read."

We get in.

"Okay," I say when I've rowed us out to the middle of the river. "Ready?"

Henry nods and I hand him the notebook.

"Wait a minute. This is a diary, not a notebook."

"I know."

"But we can't read this!" He gives it back to me.

"Why not?"

"Because it's your mom's diary!"

"But she gave it to me."

"Why?"

"Because she wanted me to read it?"

"Obviously. I just mean . . . why?"

I look out at Gus's river. "Because she wants me to know the truth," I say. "And I think this is the only way she can tell it to me. Maybe she knows this is the only way I'll listen."

He sighs. "I don't know, Bean. It seems wrong."

I hand it to him again. "She wants me to read it."

"Then what are you giving it to me for?"

"Because I can't do it."

"Do what?"

"Open it."

"Wait. You want *me* to read it? No way!"

"Why not?"

"Because it's your mom's diary!"

"Please?"

He looks down at the book sitting on his knees like he's afraid to touch it. He shakes his head. "If she gave it to you, she wants you to be the one to read it." He puts the book back on my lap.

I touch the cover again. The edges are worn.

"Go on," he says.

I hear my mom's words in my head. *It holds all the truths I have, Bean.*

But do I really want to know what they are?

Henry nods at me. "You can do it."

"Okay," I say. "Okay."

Carefully, I open the cover.

The first page is filled with doodles. Like the kind you make when you're sitting in history class and bored out of your skull.

There are faces in the squiggles. Smiley faces.

I turn the page.

More doodles.

I look up at Henry, who shrugs.

I keep flipping. Finally, I come to a page with some writing.

> I'm fifteen today.
>
> Dad gave me pearl earrings that used to be my mom's.
>
> We went out for dinner and stopped at the Italian bakery on the way home. He let me order coffee with my cannoli.
>
> When we got home, there was only one small present and I was disappointed. I opened the box and saw the earrings. When I put them on, Dad started to cry.
>
> I wish I could remember Mom wearing the earrings, but I can't.

Underneath, there's a drawing of the earrings. My earrings. I touch them in my ears. I haven't taken them out since the day I got them from my drawer. But if Gus gave them to my mom, how did I get them? And she refers to Gus as *Dad*. Dad. Not Gus.

The next two pages are filled with ears and the pearl earrings in them. No writing, just sketches.

I look up at Henry, who is glancing over the edge of the book.

"Ears?" he asks.

I shrug, touching the earrings again. I don't know why I don't want to tell him how they're important. But I keep it to myself. My stomach hurts.

The next several pages have sketches of a girl about my age. All faces. There must be about fifty. I look more closely. They aren't the same girl. It's two different girls.

Henry leans in closer.

"That looks like you."

"What? No. You're looking at it upside down."

I flip the book around so he can see.

"Yeah. You," he says. "Bet it's your mom. And the other one looks like Claire."

I turn the book back toward me again. He's right. I recognize Claire's pointy features. I flip the page.

> Claire came over again today.
> She gave me a bracelet for my birthday.
> She bought one for herself, too.
> On the inside, mine says "Best" and on hers it says "Friends."

Underneath the entry are two bracelets looped together so you can see the inscriptions. They look like rings. The next pages show more sketches of my mom and Claire's faces. Sad and happy. Tired. Angry. All different expressions. Some with captions underneath.

Best friends.
Together forever.

My mom's always been good at drawing. She's the one who writes the specials on the board at Lou's. And she's always decorated my birthday cakes and made homemade birthday cards. But these drawings are different. The details and the facial expressions are stunning. Page after page. My mom and Claire, Claire and my mom.

Soul mates.

And then a new entry with smudgy letters.

He caught us!
Oh, God.
He caught us and sent Claire home.
He hit me for the first time in my life.
He hates me.
He took all of my sheets and stuffed them
in the metal trash bin behind the garage.
He burned them.

He burned my sheets and my quilt.

The quilt my mom made for me before she died. He took back the earrings, too.

He said he was glad she died before she found out what I was.

I HATE HIM!!!!!

I stare at the tear-smudged words and put my hand over them as my throat closes up.

Oh, God.

She wasn't lying.

It holds all the truths I have, Bean.

She wasn't exaggerating. I was hoping. I was really hoping if she could almost convince herself that Bill raped her, she could have misremembered how Gus treated her, too.

"What?" Henry asks.

I shake my head.

No.

Not Gus.

Not my grandfather.

He wouldn't do that. He couldn't.

But you don't lie in your own diary. Your diary is where you write the truth.

I cover my mouth to keep from being sick. I close my eyes and lean over the book. I feel like I am twisting in a water tornado, sinking deeper and deeper into nothing but black.

"Bean! What is it?"

I shake my head. No. No. I don't believe it.

Henry leans over to look, but I cover the ugly words with my hand and turn away from him.

I want to throw the book in the river, but the pages under my hand feel alive.

Breathe. Just breathe. I force myself to turn the page. There's a large sketch of Gus's angry, hate-filled face. It's like an evil caricature of the Gus I loved. I turn the page so I don't have to look. But he's there again. And again. Page after page of Gus's rage. Uglier and uglier. I don't want to recognize him. This isn't my Gus.

But it is.

> Claire asked me to run away with her.
> But where could we go? We don't have any money. We don't even have a car.
> HE would come after me anyway.
> I will never call him Dad again.
> I STILL HATE HIM!!!

I picture my Gus acting this way. I never questioned why we called him Gus. I never knew. . . .

> Claire tried to call today.
> He ripped the phone out of the wall.
> At school today, Claire wouldn't talk to me.
> She doesn't understand why I won't run away with her.

But where would we run to?

He bought new sheets and a comforter for my bed.

Everything is purple. He thinks it's girlish, I'm sure.

Like the color will make me be the girl he wants.

I don't tell him what purple means to me.

I wish I could tell Claire.

She would die laughing.

If she would talk to me.

"Bean, you okay?"

I nod, wiping my cheeks with the back of my hand. I picture my mom's still-purple room and how she picks out purple bedding when she gets new sheets and things. I always thought she just had bad taste. But it was all about him. Still.

I got a job today at Lou's Diner.

The less time I have to be at home the better.

The next few pages are filled with sketches again. There are ugly shoes, a hairnet, a rough sketch of Lou's storefront. After that, there are pages with more doodles. Tiny sketches of flowers and some houses. The flowers remind me of the ones she decorated her dream menu with, only these are even more intricate. It seems that with each page, her drawings become more and more detailed. Beautiful. But there's something sad about them, too. This was my mom. I feel like I'm getting to know her for the first time. I touch the flowers with my fingers, imagining her drawing these when she was the same age I am now. Drawing these beautiful images while living with a man who thought she was sick. Her own father. I realize I'm getting to know him for the first time, too. And I hate it.

I look up at Henry through bleary eyes. We've drifted pretty far down the river, but I don't want to turn back. I paddle toward the center and pull the oars in again. Then turn the next page.

| *I met someone.* |

The words are surrounded by sketches of a man's face. My heart jumps.

I close the book.

"What?" Henry asks.

But my throat has closed again and I'm shaking.

He reaches for the book, but I put my hand on top of his to stop him. His hand is soft and warm and familiar. I want to keep it there and push it away at the same time.

"He's in there," I say. I knew he would be. I knew that was the main reason my mom wanted me to read the book. But suddenly it feels like too much. It's all just too much.

Our hands stay pressed together on top of the book as we float slowly down the river. With my hand on his, we're connected. We're joined somehow, and it feels like more than friendship. Like we're bonded. The question is, how? And do we really want to know?

"You have to look," he finally says, taking his hand back. "She wanted you to see."

I nod. The bottom of my hand is damp from pressing against the top of his. I open the book again and flip through the pages that came before. The squiggles and houses and faces. The horrible faces of a Gus I never knew. And then . . .

Him.

chapter twenty-four

I'm afraid he'll have my eyes. Or that he'll look exactly like me. Or Henry. But he's just a stranger looking back at me. A stranger looking over a steering wheel on one page, drinking a cup of coffee on the next. Page after page of this man. My father. Looking not at me, but away. Into the distance. You can tell my mom drew him as he was, never looking at her, but always beyond her. Maybe where he wished he could be.

He was my mom's revenge, this man. I wonder if she pictured Gus burning her things while she was with him. I wonder if she cried.

When I've seen enough, I hand the book to Henry. He studies the pages carefully, not saying a word.

I watch the houses as we float by, wondering again about the people who live inside, and what sorts of secrets they hide. I think about Gus coming out here not to get away from a noisy baby, but from a daughter he couldn't stand the sight of. And to be close to a wife who no longer existed.

The loneliness I've felt since he died turns into something darker. Something I can't name but feel desperate to get out of me. I touch the earrings in my ears and have the urge to throw them in the river. My mom never said a word about them. Never hinted that they were hers before they were mine. How could he have done that? How can my quiet, loving Gus be her angry, hateful one? How?

Finally, Henry closes the book.

"Well?" I ask.

"I don't know. It's too hard to tell."

"He doesn't look like either of us, I don't think," I say.

"No."

"He looks like he wants to escape somewhere." I look down at the water again. "I wonder where he is now."

"I don't know, Bean."

"You need to get that box."

He sighs. "I know."

"When will you get a chance, do you think?"

"Maybe tonight. She usually showers before she goes to bed. But sometimes she doesn't shower at all. Not when she's really depressed. So I don't know."

I don't answer. Imagining Sally being too depressed to wash makes my heart hurt.

"I wish I could do something," I say.

"Me too."

"I mean it."

"I know." He hands the diary to me.

"I guess we should get back," I say.

We row home without talking.

As we make our way back to the sidewalk, Mr. Clancy steps onto the path.

"Out for another joy ride?" he asks.

I nod.

"Glad the boat's not going to waste, then. Gus'd like that."

He gestures toward Henry.

"You two should have life jackets on, though. That current can be stronger than it looks. It's dangerous."

Henry looks at me for help.

"They're in the boat," I say.

"You wear 'em next time, Gus's granddaughter." He winks at me. Inside I cringe at his name for me.

"We will from now on," I say. "I promise."

He starts to turn away.

"Excuse me?" I say.

He stops and faces me again.

"Were you and Gus good friends?"

"Good friends?" He thinks a second. "No, not good friends. Acquaintances, more like. Kept to himself, mostly. Back when your grandma was alive, the two of them used to take that boat out now and then and row up and down until sunset. So sad when she died. She was a beautiful woman.

"You knew my grandmother?" I ask.

"Not to speak to. Just remember seeing them go out every so often. When you live alone like me, you notice lots of things." He smiles at me and nods. "You take care of her," he says to Henry.

Henry blushes and wipes the sweat off his forehead with the back of his hand. "I will."

"All right," Mr. Clancy says, and keeps walking.

Henry and I don't talk on the way back to my house. We stop at the edge of my driveway.

"You going to go read the rest of that?" he asks.

I nod. "Call me later? After you get the box?"

His eyebrows crinkle like they do when he gets scared or nervous. "I will."

"You can do it, Hen. It's the only way for us to get to the truth. I mean, unless we go total *Days* and get DNA tests."

"No more *Days*," he says. "We've got enough drama as it is." He smiles a little and turns and walks away.

I stand on the corner holding the diary and watch Henry trudge on down the street. He pulls his shirt away from his body three times before he's too far away for me to see.

chapter twenty-five

Inside, Claire and my mom are watching something on the Home and Garden channel. I go to the kitchen
unnoticed and make a sandwich, but I can't eat it. The
diary and the truth inside it sit on the table, waiting for
me. The earrings burn my ears. I finally give up and go to
my room. I take the earrings out and put them in their
soft, velvet case. I could give them back to my mom, but I
bet she doesn't want them any more than I do. Instead,
I go into Gus's room and put them on top of the dresser,
next to the photo I can't bear to look at. On my way out, I
shut the door.

Then I head to the roof.

It's evening now and the sun casts long, branch shadows over my place near the window. I lean back against
the steep roof and open the diary. I carefully flip through
the pages until I reach the section I left off at.

I study the sketches of my father again. Page after page

until they finally stop, and there's my mom, all by herself. There's a long section of self-portraits of my mom at my age, looking sad and alone. I look closely at her face to find traces of myself, to see what Henry saw, but I can't find a resemblance. Holding the book, I can almost feel her despair seep out of the pages and into my hands, spreading through my body. I turn another page and come to a full-body sketch of my mom. She's skinny, except for the tiny bump of her belly.

> I'm changing.
> Please don't let this be happening.
> Please let it be a mistake.

I turn another page to find more sketches of my mom and her growing stomach. My mom and me. Most pages don't have any words, but some do.

> He's gone.
> I don't know what to do.
> I'm scared.

And then nothing. Just blank pages. I flip through every one, just to make sure. But that's it. After she had me, she must have stopped.

"Beany?" My mom ducks her head out of the bathroom window. She looks different, but the same.

"We should talk now, I guess," she says.

"All right."

"Will you come in?"

I scoot over to the window and crawl through. She leads me to her room, which is all picked up, but still overwhelmingly purple. I wonder if she and Claire will redecorate it.

She sits on the edge of the bed, looking nervous. "This is hard for me," she says. "All this 'being out' stuff now. When you've kept something a secret for as long as I have, you forget how to live normal."

I stand next to her bed, looking down at her. She seems small. "Mom, you used to tell me there was no such thing as a normal childhood, remember? Well, I don't think there's such a thing as a normal anything. Especially not in this house."

She smiles. "I'm so proud of you, Bean. I'm so proud of you for being okay with this. With—me and Claire."

I remember the journal entry about Gus and cringe. I don't know how she survived it. Or how she could have stayed. If she did something like that to me, I would never stay. No matter what.

"I believe you now," I say. "About Gus. I understand why you hated him." I feel the sickness in my stomach rise again and put my hand over my mouth. I turn away from her until I can control it. "I feel like I don't know who he was anymore. Like the Gus I knew was a big lie. It feels like—like he died twice."

She waits for me to turn back to face her. "I'm so sorry. I knew it would be hard for you to read what happened.

But how could any of the rest make sense without you knowing how it all started?"

"I know," I say. "But I want to remember my Gus, too. I hate what he did to you. I do. But I can't hate him. The more I think about what happened, the more I just feel sorry for him for being so . . . ignorant. I feel sorry and, well, disappointed. And sad. Really, really sad. For everyone. But I still love him."

"I am so proud of you," she says again. "I wish I could have been half as thoughtful and forgiving as you when I was your age."

I shift uncomfortably from one foot to the other. I run through all the mean thoughts I've had about Claire since she's come into my life. "No. Don't be proud."

"I am," she says. "I know it's going to be hard. I know Claire isn't your favorite person in the world. And she hasn't exactly given you a reason to change your mind. But give her a chance. Please."

I see all the sketches of my mom and Claire together. I see the bracelet Claire gave my mom for her birthday. Best. Friends. "Mom, I—"

"Let me finish. You don't know what it's been like for her, living in . . . in secret all these years. I know that's no excuse for how she's treated you, but try to imagine what it's like to love someone and not be able to spend time with them whenever you want. To not be able to hold her hand in public. Do you know how much that hurts? What it does to you?

"I can't tell you how many times I've imagined what might have happened if Claire and I had run away together. I daydream that maybe we both could have found jobs and an apartment. And . . . oh, you know. Lived happily ever after. I know that's what Claire believed would happen. But we were just kids. We never would have made it. I knew it then and I still know it. But Claire . . . she was a dreamer. Still is. It's what I love about her. She may be rough around the edges, but that's because she's had to be. To protect herself." She sighs and shakes her head.

"When we got back together, after you were born, I was so afraid of what Gus would do if he found out. On my salary, I knew how hard it would be to raise you on my own. Heck, for the first three years of your life, I wasn't even an official 'adult.' By the time I might have been able to leave, I was so used to how things were, I was afraid to change. Maybe I felt a little safer keeping my relationship with Claire a secret. Not just from Gus, but from everyone. Claire's so much braver than I am when it comes to being okay with who you are. But me . . . not so much. Do you know when we were at the mall this week and we held hands in public for the first time someone called us dykes? I know you think the world is more open but it's not all *that* open."

I think of Claire talking with Sally in my mom's room. How happy she sounded. How she wanted to shout about my mom. How every time she looked at me, I probably reminded her that my mom had been with someone else. A guy. How could she not resent me?

"I'm sorry," I say. "I—I know it's been awful for her. For both of you. And I understand why she can't stand the sight of me."

"Oh, that's not true!"

"Um—"

"Well, okay. I admit the two of you don't get along very well. But it's nothing against you. And she'll change. I know she will!" She jumps up and hugs me. It's a tight hug. A hug like a mom would give her kid to tell her she loves her. She holds me like that for a long time, as if she wants to make sure the silent words of it will seep through to my heart. Maybe she'll never say the words again. But I feel them now, and I let them in. My hands hang awkwardly at my sides, but slowly, very slowly, I manage to slide them up and under my mom's embrace and hug her back. Her cheek is wet against mine as our tears mix together.

"Am I interrupting something?"

Claire stands in the doorway. Her spiky hair is a silhouette in the hall light.

"Yes!" my mom says, letting go with one hand and gesturing for Claire to join us.

Oh, man. I'm so not ready for this.

Claire and I exchange glances. She raises her eyebrows in question. I can almost hear the happy theme music they play on *Days* whenever someone comes back from the dead. I shrug, and Claire comes forward slowly.

"Come on, come on," my mom says encouragingly.

Claire steps into our fold. She's stiff and hard and I don't know where to put my arm, but that doesn't matter for long because my mom reaches for my hand and pulls it around Claire. She smells like laundry detergent and my mom's hair spray, only it smells different in Claire's hair. It isn't a bad smell, but it'll take getting used to.

When I can't stand it any longer, I free myself and start to head back to my room. But as I walk away, I can feel their eyes on me. I turn around. My mom sort of nudges Claire forward.

"I'm sorry," I say before she can.

She shakes her head. "You don't need to apologize."

"Yes I do," I say. I may not have said all the nasty thoughts I had about her to her face, but I still had them. She seems to understand.

"I'm sorry too," she says. And I can almost feel her apologizing for having an equal number of nasty thoughts about me.

She nods, and I nod back. I know things probably won't ever be perfect between us, but they definitely feel a lot better.

Back in my room. I open my sock drawer to put my mom's journal in it, then remember again the other journal my mom gave me. I replace one for the other and take it to my bed. It really is the exact same one as my mom's, only the lines on the front are blank. I search my room for a pen, then sit back on my bed. Carefully, I start to write.

composition book

Pearl Collatti

I stare at the name. It's so unfamiliar to me. I think about my mom and why she chose it. Of the bad turning into something good. Something valuable, even. Me. I don't really feel like a Pearl. But for the first time, I feel like something. I feel like I belong.

chapter twenty-six

I'm still in bed when the phone rings early the next morning. I grab it before my mom can.

"Hello?"

"It's me," Henry whispers.

I look around. It's slightly light out, but seems early. "What time is it? Why are you whispering?"

"Early. But I got the box."

I sit up. "Where are you?"

"Home. She's in the bathroom. I have to hurry."

"Well, look inside!"

"I can't."

"Why not?"

"I have to go. Come meet me at the MiniMart."

"Now?"

"Yeah."

"But it's—hang on." I check my clock. "Henry, it's five-thirty in the morning!"

"So what? Just meet me. I have to go!"

The phone clicks off.

I get out of bed, throw on the shorts I wore yesterday, and grab my sweatshirt. I get my mom's diary in case we need to compare sketches with a photograph or something. Then I tiptoe out of the house and make my way toward the MiniMart.

There's no sign of Henry when I get there. Even though the sun is coming up, the area still feels scary and deserted outside. I decide to go inside to wait. I pace up and down the four small aisles, past the slush machine and the Hostess rack, past the aisle with all the stuff people forget at the real grocery store, but in smaller sizes, like shampoo and toothpaste and deodorant. Past the cracker and chips aisle, where Henry and I get Sally's Doritos. Still no Henry.

The person behind the counter looks at me suspiciously, so I buy a pack of gum and continue to pace and chomp. And think. I just know if I could see Henry, I would feel the answer. If I could see him right now, I would know. But I can't, because he still hasn't showed up.

Maybe I dreamt the phone call.

I go back outside and look down the street.

Nothing.

Empty.

Forget it.

I head for Henry's house. On my way earlier, I'd rushed by on the other side of the street, just in case Sally saw me. But this time I cross the street and walk up to the front of the house, where Henry's window is.

I'm not sure what my plan is. Maybe to tap on his window and find out what's going on. But before I get there, I hear Henry yelling inside. "I'm tired of everything being a big secret! Just let me see!"

And Sally's whimper. "No."

I knock on the door and ring the doorbell. I feel like my mom, being so pushy to get in, but I don't care. I get it now. We all have to know the truth.

The yelling stops right away and Henry comes to the door. "She caught me and took the box back before I could look," he says.

"You stop it!" Sally sobs. "Beany, you go on home." She's sitting on the couch in an enormous light-yellow night-gown that looks like it used to be a brighter yellow. She's holding a red box on her lap. Her round fingers clutch it tightly. She won't face me.

I feel too uncomfortable to say anything. I'm afraid just the sound of my voice will hurt Sally. But I'm sure she needs me here. I take a deep breath and walk across the room to my spot on the couch next to her. Henry follows my lead and sits down on her other side.

Sally stares straight ahead.

My hands are shaking as I pull out the diary to the first page with Bill. I put the open book on top of the box.

"Is it him?" I ask.

A tear seeps out the corner of her eye and runs down

the same path as the ones before it, down the side of her face, along her jaw to the point of her chin. But this tear lands on my father's faraway face.

"Please, look, Sally. Please."

She sniffs and takes a deep breath. Then, very slowly, she looks down.

I hold my own breath.

I wait. She touches the tear on the man's face and smudges the black ink it was sketched in.

She turns the page.

Page after page. She keeps going even after the sketches of him end.

When she gets to the page of my pregnant mom, she keeps looking and flipping and crying.

Finally, she closes the book and hands it back to me. She sniffs again and looks at the TV, which, for the first time in my life since the hundreds—maybe thousands—of times I've been in the house, is turned off. This is her own soap. Her own story. She decides what happens next.

"Your mom," she says. She looks at Henry and then at me. "That story she made with her pictures. It could have been mine."

Could have been. My eyes meet Henry's and we tele-pathically exchange one phrase: *Thank God.*

"That man," she says. "He was just like my own Bill. My William. Just like him." Henry shifts uncomfortably.

"William," she says again. "He just left." She smoothes the top of the flat red box. "No explanation."

Henry and I watch her fingers on the box. Waiting. Gathering courage.

Slowly, they move to the gold-plated clasp that holds her secret safe, and lift the lid.

Inside, there is a handful of cards. They're the romance cards they have on the swivel rack near the checkout counter at the MiniMart. The really tacky ones that go on and on in curvy letters about true love and friendship. She opens one slowly. On the inside, above the long message, it says, "To William." And then underneath it says, "Your Sally" with a little heart.

Each one is the same.

She pulls them all out and hands them one by one to Henry, who takes them silently.

"I meant every word," she says quietly, as if she wrote them all herself.

Then, she pulls out a ribbon threaded through a thin gold band. Sally clutches it in one hand. In the other, she takes out a strip of three black-and-white photos in tiny squares. The kind you get at the arcade. "We eloped so I don't have any wedding pictures," Sally explains. "Just this." Two faces smile drunkenly out at the world. Sally, her face much thinner, her hair jet black and pulled away from her eyes in a barrette, smiling like I've never seen her smile. And a stranger. He has a mustache and glasses and lighter hair. He looks older. He's serious, even though he's sort of smiling, looking away and beyond, like he has somewhere else to go. Just like the man in my mom's diary. But different. He's different.

Sally's William is not my mom's Bill.

Sally brings the photo strip to her chest and presses it there as she sobs. When the photo touches her heart, she cries even harder.

Henry and I put our arms around her at the same time so that our arms cross as we hold her, together, and let her cry.

chapter twenty-seven

When Sally finishes, Henry gets some tissues.

"I'm sorry, Beany," she says as she wipes her face.

"Don't be," I say. I want to tell her I understand, but I don't want to embarrass her. Besides, who knows if I really understand anything at all?

"It's just so hard not knowing."

I nod.

"For months I was sure he was killed in a crash or something. Or kidnapped. It had to be something like that. I called all the hospitals to see if he'd been admitted. I called the police. But when they came to the house, I knew what they were thinking. Of course he left. Why would he stay with a lady like me?"

"Don't, Mom," Henry says.

"Ah, Hen. It's okay." She slowly puts all the cards back in the box.

I wonder how she got them back from William. Then I realize he must have left them behind.

"Of course I must have known somehow that he left on purpose," Sally says. "Of course I must have. His car was gone. He took all his clothes and things. The only things he left were—" She hugs the box. "Well. He didn't leave me much. Just my own broken heart."

Henry looks at his lap.

Sally leans forward and puts the box on the coffee table.

"I'm sorry," I say. It sounds lame, but I have to say something.

She nods. "I just have to accept that he's gone and I'll never know exactly why. But a man who does that is no good. I spent a lot of time—years—thinking he'd show up with some explanation, and we'd all be happy again. But you know? I'm starting to realize maybe we were never happy. It's not like TV. In real life, people don't come back. Sorry, Hen. But that's the truth. I have to face the fact that he's gone forever. He's not your secret spy, and he didn't get killed on a special mission."

Henry and I exchange guilty looks.

"He's a deadbeat who didn't want the responsibility of being a dad. Just like your daddy, Bean girl. You and Henry just got unlucky in the daddy department. But look how nice you both turned out anyway."

She puts her soft hands on both our thighs and

squeezes. I believe I can feel part of Henry's gladness seep through her hand, into her heart, down her other arm, and out her other hand onto me.

"I guess we all need to head on over to your house, Beany, and tell your mom the news. But first, I need to clean up."

She stands slowly, as if the heavy thing is still inside her. Her nightgown sticks to her a bit and shows the folds of fat on her back. Henry instinctively pulls the material away from her body.

"Thanks, Hen," she says. "I won't be long."

She toddles down the hallway to the bathroom and shuts the door. Soon we hear the water running.

The large space between Henry and me feels enormous. Sally has sat there for so long and so often there's actually a big dip there. It feels like a canyon we have to cross to get to one another again.

We sit and listen to the water running in the bathroom.

And then, finally, Henry clears his throat and we turn to look at each other. And when we do, it is the same Henry I've always known and loved. My best friend. But there's something different, too. Something that makes my stomach feel strange and wonderful. He shifts closer to me so he's halfway in the dent. I shift closer to him so that I'm halfway in it, too. And then we both allow gravity to let us fall toward each other until our faces are so close I have to close my eyes and hope for the best.

And the best is what happens next.

In all the times I imagined my first real kiss, I never thought it would involve the lips of my best friend, Henry.

Sometimes I think it's best when the dreams you've lived with all your life get scrambled around and come out all mixed up and crazy.

We kiss and hold each other and let the magic of the moment race through our hearts, through our arms, our legs, our fingers and toes. When the shower stops, we pull away from each other instinctively. Henry looks surprised and scared. It's sort of like looking in a mirror because he looks exactly the way I feel. But as I start to smile, his mouth turns up just as slowly as mine does. Until we're both smiling and pulling ourselves out of Sally's cavern.

When Sally finally comes back down the hall, she's dressed in a new outfit. Probably one she bought with my mom and Claire. She's done her hair up in a tasteful French twist sort of thing. She looks more alive than I've ever seen her.

"I'm ready," she says. She leads the way outside and down the street.

Henry and I walk side by side, letting our hands brush against each other every so often. I can barely feel the pavement under my feet. I don't realize I'm still smiling until I look over at Henry and see him grinning like a fool.

When we get to my house, Sally pauses to take some calming breaths.

"It'll be fine," I tell her. "My mom will be relieved you aren't mad anymore. I promise."

I go up the stairs first and open the door.

"Mom?" I call out.

There's no response.

"I'll be right back," I say.

I run inside and look around but no one is up yet. When I get to the top of the stairs, a loud noise comes from my mom's room—a huge clunk. Then giggling.

My mom's door is open. I hesitate, then step closer.

"I think we broke the bed!" my mom whispers loudly.

"Mom?" I say from the hallway.

"Oh, crap!"

More hysterical giggling.

"Just a sec, hon!"

Oh, lord. Did I really just catch my mom and Claire doing it?

I lean against the wall and shudder, trying to clear the image from my mind. This is going to be so hard to get used to. My mom. Having sex. There are just some things you don't want to imagine your mom doing no matter who it's with.

I shake my head to clear the thought.

"I'll be downstairs," I say loudly. "Sally and Henry are here! Everything's cool now!"

"Okay, honey!" my mom calls. Then they both burst out laughing again.

And I can't help it.

I shake my head again and laugh too. That's when I

notice Gus's open door. I don't look inside when I pass by, but I pause for just a moment.

Be good.

I can almost hear the trace of his voice. See the way he looked at me with love and concern. And I know at least that part of him was sincere. *Don't worry, Gus,* I think to myself. *I'll be fine.*

chapter twenty-eight

That night, in the living room, we're all together again. Claire and my mom sit on the floor down in the front, leaning against the coffee table. My mom has her arm around Claire's shoulder, and Claire leans her head into my mom's neck. They seem to be a necessary part of one another, one supporting the other like that. They sit so naturally side by side, as if it's always been that way. I don't know if Claire and I will ever really like each other, but if she makes my mom happy, I guess I can cope.

On the coffee table sits a large metal mixing bowl half-filled with popcorn covered with sugar, melted butter, and salt.

Gus's empty chair has been pushed to the corner and out of the way. I think I will always wonder if maybe he could have come around and accepted my mom and Claire. I know my mom's opinion on that, but I like to imagine maybe there was a chance. Maybe he even could have been sorry.

Sally sits on the sofa right between Henry and me. We're watching *An Affair to Remember* again. Claire and my mom insisted. This time, I really get it. I know why the story means so much to my mom and Claire. And, after what Henry and I have been through, to us, too. When we get to the end where Nicky and Terry are in Terry's apartment and Nicky puts all the pieces together and runs into Terry's bedroom and sees the portrait Nicky made of her wearing his grandmother's shawl, I have to admit that I'm crying just a little.

I watch the back of Claire's and my mom's heads. Claire raises her hand to her face at the same time as my mom to wipe away Claire's tears. Sally sighs heavily and wipes her own face with a pink tissue she's pulled from a pocket in her dress. There is no question in my mind that this scene blows away any love scene from *Days of Our Lives*. I reach over and touch Sally's leg, and she puts her puffy hand on mine, balled-up tissue and all. She gives my hand a very gentle squeeze that makes everything feel even more all right. I pretend she's sending me a message in that squeeze. That she hasn't given up hope. She still believes in love. All kinds. Even her own.

When the credits start to roll, Henry stands and heads toward the kitchen. I pick up my glass and drink what's left for an excuse to follow him.

In the kitchen light, Henry's face glistens in the summer night heat. He smiles shyly at me. When I place my empty glass on the counter, my hand is shaking.

I pull it back and hold my elbows, feeling suddenly more uncomfortable in front of Henry than I have in my entire life.

We spend what feels like ages not looking at each other. But I can feel some sort of gravitational pull forcing our eyes to find each other. And when I look into his, I suddenly feel myself being sucked into this sort of time travel. Scenes of our childhood flash through my mind like a tacky soap opera montage. I see Henry smiling at me the first day we met at the MiniMart, a box of Suzy Q's and a copy of *Soap Opera Digest* tucked under each arm as he searched in his pocket for the money Sally'd given him to pay for their treats. I see him at school, looking down at his clean shoes, hurrying through the hallways, trying not to be noticed. I see him again and again, waiting for me at the MiniMart so I can buy my mom's Snickers and coffee and he can buy Sally's Doritos. I see him at the door as we stand outside my house, just before we learn about Gus. I see him by the river with me, brushing ashes off our legs and then tossing what we can into the hot air. I see him not laughing when everyone else did. I see his sad, understanding eyes. I see him on the boat, looking in the water for answers that aren't there. On the couch, comforting Sally about a man she never really knew. And I see him now, looking at me. Waiting.

I have always loved Henry. From the moment we met. He's like my brother. But he isn't. He is my best friend. And now . . . now . . . What is he now?

I put my hand back on the counter to steady myself. I force myself not to turn away from him. And it feels as though he's doing the same thing. Watching and waiting. Wondering.

I concentrate on my heart and the new way it's beating—has been beating since our first kiss. The way it hurts and feels wonderful at the same time. For just a second, I let my eyes move to his chest where his heart is.

Henry pulls at his shirt self-consciously.

The music from the credits is playing in the other room. There isn't much time.

I think of my mom in the truck with my dad and that faraway look on his face in every single sketch. How he looked gone before he even left.

I think of Henry's dad in the picture with Sally and how he had the same expression. He was somewhere else already, too.

But here is Henry. Looking at me. Not in the faraway distance. He is right here. Just like he always has been.

I think of the photograph of my grandparents and how happy they look. How their love is so obvious and natural and real.

And I imagine me and Henry in a photo. How we might look if someone captured our faces right at this moment. I can see us. Best friends. Just the way my grandparents were. Two people who understand each other perfectly and love each other because of it.

We move closer to each other at the same time.

"Henry," I say. The name sounds funny, as if I've never said it out loud. It isn't a question. Just . . . Henry. Because he's here.

"Yes," he says. He blushes.

And then we both start to laugh. We laugh as if laughing is something we've never done before. And the way it fills me up, the way our laughter blends together so we sound like one person, means we don't have to say anything at all. Because it's a laughter filled with relief and gratitude, the friendship of a lifetime, and the hope of a future. It's the laugh of a promise that doesn't require words. It's a laugh filled with love.

I reach my arms out to his shoulders to steady myself. And he does the same to me. And we keep on laughing until I have to rest my head on his chest and he has to put his arms around me and press his face into my hair, and we hold each other up and become quiet. Quiet, and happy, and ready for the next episode in our lives.